CIRCUS

CLAIRE BATTERSHILL

CIR

CUS

McCLELLAND & STEWART

Library and Archives Canada Cataloguing in Publication

Battershill, Claire
Circus / Claire Battershill.

ISBN 978-0-7710-1278-5

I. Title.

PS8603.A877C57 2013 C813'.6 C2012-904046-0

Printed and bound in the United States of America

McClelland & Stewart,
a division of Random House of Canada Limited
A Penguin Random House Company
One Toronto Street
Suite 300
Toronto, Ontario
M5C 2V6
www.randomhouse.ca

1 2 3 4 5 18 17 16 15 14

 *For Terence, with thanks for the beginning.* 

Damn everything but the circus! . . . damn everything that is grim, dull, motionless, unrisking, inward turning, damn everything that won't get into the circle, that won't enjoy, that won't throw its heart into the tension, surprise, fear and delight of the circus, the round world, the full existence . . .

– e.e. cummings

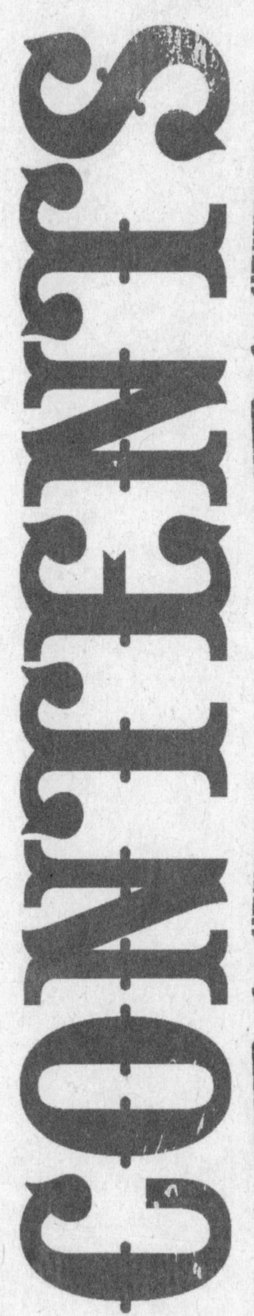

CONTENTS

A GENTLE LUXURY

☞ HENRY BOTTLESWORTH HAS GIVEN HIMSELF thirty-one days to find love on the Internet. For the past ten years, his friends and relations have been setting him up with their co-workers, friends of friends, sisters' friends, former schoolmates, and second cousins. Henry has dutifully attended every date and allowed himself a carefully measured dose of optimism each time. He always takes note of buffed fingernails, a well-loved purse, or a hand-knit scarf and saves these details for later, just in case. Too polite to refuse his friends' matchmaking efforts, he has sat through more silences punctuated by bouts of awkward eating than he cares to count.

Henry has, with time and experience, learned a thing or two about the culinary ins and outs of first dates. Sushi, for instance, invites a rice explosion. Ordering a saucy noodle dish or a dressing-laden salad is asking for a spill, and Chinese broccoli is impossible to eat all in one bite without losing one's dignity. In his own way, Henry has become an expert in the etiquette of courtship:

Never wear a white shirt.

Never arrive early.

Never arrive late.

Never ask about previous relationships.

Never forget to bring your wallet.

Always keep mints or gum in your pocket.

These are common-sense rules, and most people seem to emerge from the womb knowing them. Henry, however, has educated himself solely through trial and error, with a heavy emphasis on error. Sometimes, though, he learned more than one lesson on a single date. Sushi, therefore, is forever associated with the memory of spending an entire evening attempting to conceal a soy sauce stain on the breast pocket of his white button-down by crossing his arms in an uncomfortably lofty position over his chest, followed by the shame of reaching into his back pocket to find it empty of both wallet and gum. Not that minty-fresh breath would have really been necessary at that point. The Age of Matchmaking, he's decided, has now come to an end.

On one particularly embarrassing occasion Henry's younger brother Charles was careless in his role as Cupid, and forgot to tell both Henry and Bachelorette #1 – Penelope, who had just moved to London from Minneapolis to begin her degree in anthropology – that they had been invited to his flat in order to be set up. Henry spent most of the evening in the kitchen, occupying himself by sipping gin from a plastic cup, nibbling on cheese-and-onion-flavoured crisps, and pouring drinks for first-year students who assumed he was a hired bartender, rather than dancing in sock feet in his brother's living room with a rabble of sweaty eighteen-year-old strangers. Penelope, on the other hand, had literally let her hair down, and was bouncing up and down in the middle of the crowd of bodies, whipping her long, messy curls about to the rhythm of "Common People" as if she were in an advert for volumizing shampoo. Charles would not give up on the idea of pairing them, however, and kept physically pushing the two together until Penelope and Henry finally bumped foreheads in the kitchen doorway, leaving him with an unsightly goose egg above his left eyebrow and her with a mild concussion. Accidental head-butts do not often lead to intimacy, but in the decade since that party, Penelope and Henry have become the kind of friends whose hearts leap for each other, so that they just have to sit close together, Penny's head resting on Henry's shoulder, to be perfectly content.

That first night, he had fetched some ice and wrapped it up in a tea towel to apply to her forehead, and they'd sat on the stairs leading out of Charles's flat. Penelope leaned on his shoulder and twirled her index finger around a strand of her hair, and told him over and over again that she would probably leave soon, but made no motions to go until he stood up himself. Henry had liked her from the start, and for whatever reason she was fond of him, too, even if it was somehow clear to both of them from their first meeting that romance was not a possibility.

Since blind dates failed to lead to actual amorousness, Henry finally swore off them. For a time, he had given up on love altogether in pursuit of other fine things in life. He home-brewed beer in his bathtub, obsessively cultivated a small lemon tree that he impulse-purchased at a street market, took daytrips to stately homes operated by the National Trust on weekends, and pondered the minor everyday concerns of his job – a reasonably respectable position in the Foreign Office. It's not that he's discontented being on his own – the hobbies are certainly fulfilling – it's simply that he has now decided to try his hand at Internet dating, within sensible limits.

One month is the free-trial period for the matchmaking website run by a London newspaper. While Henry has unshakeable faith in his new quest for love, he doesn't want it to become an unhealthy preoccupation, nor does he wish to pay the absurd fee of twenty-five pounds and sixty pence per month for the privilege of using a website. He chose the month of October, with its thirty-one full days, in order to get the most out of his free trial. Even in a leap year, February is not a good choice. Then there's the additional minefield of Valentine's Day, to be avoided on first dates and in the delicate early days of a relationship. No indeed. October is optimal. There is the added bonus that, this being London, it will probably rain every single day in October, so Henry hopes to have the opportunity to perform some act of gallantry by sharing his jacket or umbrella, or carrying his date across a puddle to save her shoes.

On the last day of September, Henry asks Penny to meet for coffee so he can tell her all about his scheme. She is one friend who has never played the matchmaking game with him. Her first question is a surprise. It turns out that just as in the early days of his dating education he hadn't anticipated the perils of soggy salad and unruly noodles, he also hasn't considered some of the basic principles of Internet-dating strategy.

"What are you going to do about a photo?"

"A photo?"

"You need a picture, right?" A thin moustache made of milk appears briefly on her upper lip before she licks it off.

"Oh, I hadn't really given it any thought."

"The photo is the heart of the dating profile, Henry." She pauses to drink her latte and tries not to giggle. "With the right photo you can say it all: are you fun, are you serious, are you handsome, are you thin, are you fat, are you nerdy, are you carefree, are you charming, are you quirky? What are you? It can give you everything or take it all away."

"Is that not a bit superficial? There are loads of questions, and one even receives compatibility scores. Surely, those are the answers that matter?"

"Not if the photo sucks."

In the ensuing silence, Henry tries to think of the most flattering camera angles and finds he is unfailingly picturing himself in a trilby hat, although he has never worn one in his life. He takes a slow bite of his croissant and gazes at Penny as pleadingly as he can. She taps his shin under the table with the toe of her boot.

"You know, some people have professional consultations about this stuff. There are services for that now."

"Honestly?"

"Not that I'm suggesting you need to do that. I'm just saying that it's a big deal, and what you definitely can't do, though I can tell that you're thinking about it, is leave out the photo. Anything they're left to imagine will be more horrifying than you could possibly ever look in a photograph."

"Perhaps this is more your domain?"

"I'll work on it," Penny says as she begins ransacking her purse in search of something small. "For now, you come up with some witty answers for the personality quiz and decide what you think about open relationships."

"Daunting, really. All this."

"No cold feet. I think it's a perfect idea! All you need is a little practise. Courtship is, after all, an art form like any other." She extracts her wallet and places it on the table.

"Says she, the Master?"

"Hey! I am very happy, I'll have you know." Penny reaches across the table and laces her fingers through Henry's. "Very happy." She glances fleetingly down at their hands and then grabs the bill. "This one's on me."

When they leave the café it is raining prodigiously and neither of them has an umbrella. Henry takes off his blazer and drapes it over both of their heads, and they lope along, laughing and stumbling, as though they're in a three-legged race, to the entrance of the underground.

"By the way," she says, when they get into the station, "you know those trial things are usually thirty days from when you open your account, right? You don't have to choose a calendar month. The clock could start any time."

"And, knowing this, you still let me explain my genius October plan?"

"You can still start on the first," she says, kissing him on the cheek. She slips a sweet she's taken from the café into the pocket of his jacket as she hands it back to him. They part ways at the turnstile and get on separate trains going in different directions. In the crowded carriage, Henry looks out the window at the dark insides of the tunnel. For the first time in their ten years of friendship, he wonders if perhaps he was wrong about Penelope. He wonders, that is, if he loves her.

When he returns to the office, Henry changes into a dry shirt in anticipation of his afternoon meeting. Every week, he has the same appointment on Thursday afternoon at three o'clock. With few exceptions he has been in the same place at the same time doing the same thing for seven years' worth of Thursdays. The person he meets is unfailingly five minutes late and always refuses the coffee he offers. Her name is Alexandra Papadakis, and she comes to meet with him on behalf of the Greek embassy. She is not beautiful, but there is a kind of charming mousiness to her, and in spite of their weekly confrontation, Henry has come to feel the kind of fondness for her that he might feel for a hopeless niece. He doesn't know quite how old she is, though he assumes – hopes, even – that she is younger than he is. Mostly, he is curious about her life, about what she thinks about when she gets home from work, and what she does with her hair when it isn't in a bun. He imagines she's the type of person who knits and reads books about paper crafts and makes fruit preserves and seldom watches television, but has, in spite of these virtuous pastimes, never had a true talent. It is very clear that Alexandra does not share Henry's platonic affection.

When Ms. Papadakis enters his office at 3:05 that afternoon, he notices she has wet patches on the elbows of her suit jacket where her small umbrella didn't quite cover her. As she sits down slowly in the chair opposite his desk, he is met once again by her freakishly large green eyes, which look like those of a Tarsier. He means this comparison to what he considers the world's most adorable primate to be a compliment, but somehow he's sure Ms. Papadakis wouldn't see it the same way. If he has learned nothing else, dating has taught him to keep such thoughts to himself.

Every week she has the same question for him, and every week he gives the same answer.

"Can we have our Marbles back?" asks Alexandra, again.

"No," says Henry, again.

They sit for a moment without saying anything, and then Alexandra stands and runs her hands over her skirt, smoothing the creases. She blinks too often, and she has an unconscious habit of biting her bottom lip repeatedly.

"Thank you for your time, Mr. Bottlesworth. I will see you next week. We might have a new proposal for you then." She always says something like this, some cold promise designed to show her professionalism and seriousness. Perhaps some day she will get a promotion.

"Have a lovely week, Alexandra," he says as he stands and extends his hand across his desk.

In reply, she shakes out her umbrella onto Henry's carpet and leaves the office without saying goodbye. Henry sits back down and fiddles with his email. Despite the long-standing nature of their predicament, Henry and Alexandra have never once made a joke about their situation. They have never commented on the predictability of the exchanges, as each week they earnestly say their lines, act their parts, and then exit the stage. The Marbles they're disputing are the Elgin Marbles, priceless classical Greek sculptures that once formed part of the Parthenon. They were plundered by English collectors in the 1800s, when looting the precious goods of other cultures was commonplace, and now exist in a purpose-built gallery in the British Museum. Keats wrote a poem about gazing at them, and Henry has the little piece of verse pinned to his office bulletin board, as if the Romantic poet had somehow claimed English ownership of these Marbles better than anyone else ever could. Better than Henry himself. Greece wants the Marbles back and England will never, ever give them up, partly on account of the bespoke museum gallery and partly as a matter of national pride. Finders keepers, and so on. But it is Alexandra's job to keep asking, and it is Henry's job to say no.

Henry doesn't tell many people about this side of his work, because there is a part of him that is embarrassed to admit that his job could be done as well, or perhaps even better, by a note pinned to his door that says "NO" in bold, aggressive lettering. Sometimes, after a couple of drinks and when he is feeling particularly confident about his place in the world, he is able to pull off the story as a party anecdote, but usually that involves a lengthy explanation about the history of the Elgin Marbles, which is, Henry has learned from sad experience, very few people's idea of a good time. He had denied Alexandra's sole request several times before he actually went to see the Marbles himself. He couldn't quite muster Keats's sublime feeling about the passing of time and the imminence of death, but the Marbles were quite impressive, it was true, and somehow tragic. Alone in the gallery, Henry did feel a little "like a sick eagle looking at the sky," but then that particular phrase from the Keats poem described his entire way of being in the world, and not just how he felt when confronted with exquisitely old things in a museum. He had walked the length of the gallery, hoping to discover what the carved faces and the surfaces of the stone could tell him, to figure out what he was working to protect. What he wanted more than anything was to touch them, as though he were a little boy encountering the bones of a Tyrannosaurus Rex for the first time. He didn't touch anything at all, of course, for fear of setting off an alarm, and instead made his exit, leaving the Marbles to their eternity.

Henry does not consider himself a literary person, and hasn't read a poem since he was forced to read them at school. The Keats, however, he memorized and contemplated and tried to understand until he could hardly bear to think about it anymore. He believed it was part of his duty, although no one at work had told him so. He recited the poem to Penny one day and a funny expression came over her face, as though she was sorry for something. She hadn't said anything afterward, had simply stayed quiet. He wasn't sure if she was having big feelings about art and mortality or just acting appropriately reverent at the sound of the sonnet. Although he had not said the poem out loud again, sometimes "the rude / Wasting of old time – " ran through his head without warning while he polished his shoes.

As Henry leaves the office on the first day of October, after spending the afternoon sending a dozen useless emails and filling out some forms, he prepares himself for the task of writing his online profile. What will he do about a likeness? He hadn't been worried about it initially, but now that he knows professional services exist to fashion ideal profiles, perhaps he ought to make more of an effort? Though he continues to ponder suitable haberdashery for a good first impression, he is sure anyone who is interested in his appearance alone is not to be trusted.

When he arrives at his flat, Henry makes himself a cup of tea and sits down at the computer. The first questions are easy to answer, such as his name, age, gender, and sexual orientation. On the next screen, Henry is confronted with a list of seventy-eight questions, his answers to which will, apparently, give him a score and generate a personality profile so that he can be matched with individuals who have given compatible answers to the same questions. Henry drinks his tea and prepares to be assessed. He types:

Angry Birds.

Not likely.

A weakness for strong cheddar.

To Canada once, when I was a boy.

Twilight. I just needed to know what the fuss was about.

Half full.

Winston Churchill.

The questions appear to be in a perplexingly random order. Still, he works his way down the list, answering quickly, honestly, and instinctively. Some of the questions are covertly intimate and sexual (Q: "Rough or gentle?" A: "Gentle."), and some are frivolous and seemingly irrelevant (Q: "Have you ever been to the London Aquarium?" A: "No."). What kind of person is he, based on these answers? He begins to regret his hasty approach.

He uploads a photo Penny took of him during a winter stroll in Kensington Gardens. In the snapshot, he is wearing a winter hat and a duffel coat and laughing, his eyes wrinkled at the corners, while glancing slightly away from the camera. He suspects that the photo will at least attract women who like happy men, and he will come across as what he might describe – if he were writing an old-fashioned personal ad – as carefree and fun-loving. When he eventually hits "submit," the webpage takes a minute to load before presenting him with a series of compatible matches. Henry gets up and goes to the kitchen to warm up his tea as a measure of procrastination. When he returns to his computer, he sees an overwhelming number of smiling, thumbnail-sized women. The highest compatibility match is 63 per cent, and Henry has no idea if this is a good or a bad sign. He opens up the first profile on the list: Robin Kendry, a librarian who has four cats and lives in Devon. His allergies rule that one out, so he scrolls down, browsing the coquettish poses and made-up faces. He picks up the phone beside his computer.

"I don't think I can do this."

"That bad? How far did you get?" Penny's voice is hoarse.

"I made my profile and now my screen is full of potentially dateable women."

"Right. Which picture did you use?"

"Kensington."

"I was going to suggest that one. Look, I have to go, sorry."

Henry hears Garry in the background, asking who it is. Penny doesn't reply. "Maybe just call it a night and we can go through the profiles together tomorrow? Lunch at that place that does free wireless?"

"See you at twelve-thirty, then."

Penny has dated a number of men (and one woman) since she and Henry became friends all those years ago, and her partners have always been more interested in her than she has been in them. For a while, when she was in university, Henry could hardly keep track of their names, after having been introduced to what seemed to him like an endless succession of polo enthusiasts, thespians, future politicians, and semi-professional tennis players. When Garry, with his broad, muscular shoulders and his high-stress job in finance, had stayed on the scene longer than the rest, and eventually moved into Penny's flat a year ago, Henry assumed that, as the two most important men in her life, they would become friends. Instead, Garry tends to check his emails on his phone while Henry and Penny practise their falsetto singing along with The Darkness or watch *Amélie* again. He closes his eyes for a moment. When he opens them, he is faced once again with the miniature portraits on his screen.

Online dating is the right thing to do. It must be.

When Henry arrives at the café for lunch the next day, Penny is already sitting by the window with her laptop open. She is unusually pale and wearing an oversized knitted sweater with leggings.

"Don't come too close," she says in a rough voice, gesturing at the chair across from, rather than beside her.

"Feeling poorly?" Henry asks, still standing.

Penny nods.

"Well, you needn't have come for my sake. Shouldn't you be in bed?"

"I wouldn't miss the start of your romantic adventures. Anyway, what would I do in bed all day aside from feel miserable? I might as well have a distraction."

"Right, then. Here we are."

As he settles into the seat opposite Penny, Henry silently wishes that she hadn't come. He is fervently fearful about illness, and absolutely does not want to catch whatever she has. He feels repelled and ashamed all at the same time – perhaps he is the worst friend the world has ever known for being so fickle, when only the other day he was gazing at her and wondering if she was the hidden love of his life. Now he cannot think of anything less appealing than kissing her.

"I'll have the soup," Penny orders, as Henry logs on to the dating site on her laptop.

Henry orders a chicken sandwich and when he turns his attention back to the laptop, his own face smiles up at him from the screen. "Here's my bit." Henry turns the computer towards her.

Penny leans over the table and points to the yellow star at the edge of the page. "You have a message! Go on, open it!" she says, before lapsing into a coughing fit that rattles her chest. Henry does his best not to wince as he runs his finger across the doubtless germ-covered trackpad of her computer. He begins to read aloud.

"Linda Rosenberg says, 'Want to get together? I am American. I work as a waitress in Camden. See my profile for details. Let's meet, semi-colon, close bracket, less-than symbol, three?' Wait, what does that punctuation mean?"

Penny laughs. "It's a wink and a heart! You've made quick work of it all, haven't you? Don't you think this is exciting?"

"Seems a bit much, doesn't it?"

"It's a dating site. She's supposed to be forward. Here. Let's check out her profile."

The food arrives and Henry excuses himself so he can wash his hands before picking up his sandwich. He washes them three times with antibacterial soap before he feels satisfied. When he returns, Penny is peering intently at the computer screen.

"She's super pretty," Penny says, turning the computer back to face Henry.

"Unfeasibly beautiful," he agrees.

"So? You only have thirty days, right? You might as well answer."

Henry takes the computer and composes a terse, matter-of-fact reply to Linda Rosenberg's message, suggesting coffee at a bakery near his flat next Saturday at two p.m. She is a vision in her white blouse and rosy cheeks and voluminous hair, and he is certain that as soon as she sees him in the flesh it will all be over, but he presses "send." Perhaps she will turn out to be as kind as she is pretty, and then he can stop Internet dating and just love her.

"Just one other reason I wanted to have lunch today," Penny says, watching him as she picks at her fingernails. "Although, you're right, I should have stayed in bed." She contemplates her hands and her messy gathering of hair flops to one side in what would under other circumstances be a comical way. "Garry slept behind the couch last night."

"Why would he do that?"

"He's been seeing someone else." Penny sniffles into a tissue.

Henry simultaneously wants to hug Penny and punch Garry, so he settles for tapping the table weirdly with his fist. "Bloody. Fucking. Bastard!"

"No, don't worry, Henry. It's just this cold. I'm not really that upset, somehow. I guess there was part of me that must have thought about the possibility of things going south. But it was nice, you know? No need to ruin it by getting all dramatic about the ending. I let him stay the night, but I didn't want him on the furniture." She clears her throat, which sounds as though it is full of stones. "He smelled amazing. That's how I knew. I mean, Garry dresses pretty well, he takes care of himself, but he doesn't usually smell like jasmine, you know?"

She's aiming to make him laugh, but Henry feels so unsettled and unable to help her that he lets out a strange wheeze instead. Henry watches her as she tells the whole story, as she stares out the window and makes an unsuccessful attempt to rearrange her hair. He struggles to quiet his rage at Garry long enough to think of reassuring things to say, but can't bring himself to interject in case what he does say is the wrong thing. Best just to be here, he decides, and listen for as long as she'll have him.

"But it's fine. I'm good. I really did know all the time it wasn't a 'forever' thing. So I'm good. I'm good. I'm not worried about it."

Henry still has no idea what to do, so he gets up and sits beside Penny and puts his arm around her. She leans into his shoulder and tries to suppress a cough. "I'm sorry. I know how you feel about sick people. You've been worrying this whole time about catching my cold. And now I think I might be feverish."

Henry feels her forehead with the back of his hand, kisses the top of her head, and snuggles her closer. "Yes, a raging temperature. But for you, at a time like this, even I can overlook a virus," he says, feeling nauseous. He tucks her wild hair behind her ears and closes her laptop with his free hand. "Let me take you home and put you to bed."

As they walk back to her flat, Henry holds Penny's hand. They don't speak. They cut through Hyde Park and there are geese by the pond, dipping their webbed feet in the water and honking like maniacs. There aren't many people out, since it's not terribly warm, and everything seems grey, the hedges and the flowers and especially Penny's fingers, which must be getting cold. It's probably a longer stroll than she can comfortably manage in her condition, but it's too late now, they're between tube stations. Henry reassures himself that the fresh air will do her good.

When they turn the corner onto Penny's street, Henry nudges her, checking in. She gives him a slightly trembling thumbs-up. Henry tries to distract himself by worrying about Linda Rosenberg and what he'll wear and what time he'll have to leave to meet her. What kind of coffee-shop pastry can be consumed with grace? Perhaps he will throw caution to the wind and choose something rich, messy, and sweet. But all the

Linda Rosenbergs cease to matter as he wraps his arm around Penny's shoulders so that they hit an even rhythm in their shared stride, as if they've practised walking together every day of their lives.

SENSATION

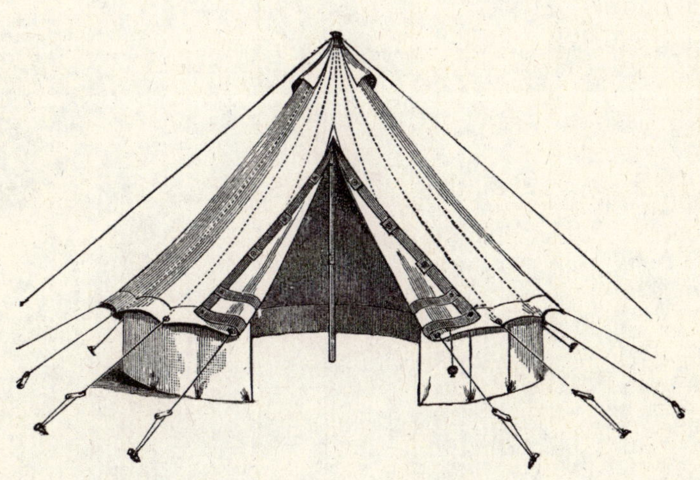

ANNIE LOVES IT. SHE CAN'T GET ENOUGH. She could stare and stare at the blue of it all day, just lying on her back with her eyes wide open. There are not many things Annie loves as much as this blue. She loves how the energy-saver light bulb glows like a dying star through the waterproof nylon, how scents from the rest of the house filter in, from time to time, through the mesh windows. She loves the plasticky smell of it, too, and the feel of the carpet through the sturdy plastic on the ground, the way she can stick her sock feet out the front if she wants to. She is open to the elements, but there's no danger of rain or mosquitoes, no need for thermal underwear or finicky gas lanterns. This is camping at its finest.

✶

They pitched the pale-blue tent in the living room on the morning of Annie's sixteenth birthday. They thought they'd just try it out, to make sure it was as simple to assemble as the box promised. Annie and her father moved the sofa over and rolled up the rug to create a perfect spot beside the window. And voilà! They had never imagined how easy! Twist the spokes into place and up it goes with a sound like an unusually hearty sneeze. It seemed almost a genuine miracle, compared with the tents of yore – of Annie's father's youth. That kind took an army of boy scouts an entire day to assemble, and then a separate army of their overbearing mothers and woodsy fathers another full day to put away. But not this tent. Annie's tent opened itself to the living room like one of those tropical flowers that blooms, suddenly, when the sun goes down.

Annie's dad, Jake, has never been very good at birthday presents, but this time he got it right. He googled "tents for teenagers" and then embarked on a long Internet excursion involving religious camping experiences for youth-at-risk and Bible study sites that listed fourteen different interpretations of the same line of verse. He liked the archaic-sounding translations best – they made the very notion of a tent sound worthy: "Enlarge the place of thy tent, and let them stretch forth the curtains of thine habitations" (Isaiah 54:2). Eventually, he regained his focus and found a site with a tent selector tool. He chose the number of people it needed to sleep from a drop-down menu (1–3); the difficulty of set-up (very easy); the degree of waterproofing (medium is always a good bet, right?). Four possible tents appeared on the screen. The only question missing from the tool was something about the appropriateness for the occasion, though PattiC from Minnesota had written in the comments section that she had thrown an outdoor-themed slumber party for her sixteen-year-old, which had been a "roaring success." Jake wrote down the model number and went to the store.

Along with the tent, he gave Annie a new sleeping bag and a little flashlight and some freeze-dried astronaut food from the space museum, in case she was ever lost in the wilderness and needed something to sustain her for hunting and gathering. When they first popped the tent up, it was Jake who was most excited. "Isn't this neat?" He touched the convergence of poles lightly with the tips of his fingers, as if it might fall down at the slightest provocation. "You can have real shelter, just like that!" he said, snapping his fingers with a satisfying crack. Snapping was one of his best skills. "And it all fits in here! You could carry it in one hand!" He picked up the tent's tiny mesh stuff-sac and dangled it from his wrist to demonstrate. He could hardly believe the technological innovation in outdoor gear since he had traipsed uncomfortably through the woods with Annie's mother all those years ago. He had carried heavy steel poles and the enormous canvas tent and all the provisions himself, nearly blowing out his back without asking Annie's mother to help bear the load. They fought for nearly three hours about how to put up the tent, each having a particular notion of how it should look when it was fully assembled and where exactly the ground was flattest. When Annie's mother grew tired of arguing, she lit a cigarette and sat on a rotting log while he held two incompatible poles from the frame, one in each hand, and tried to piece them together. She had never been interested in camping, had come mainly to please him. Before she met Jake, she had never even had a s'more, which he thought was a travesty. But when he made one for her, she took a single bite, shrugged, and threw the rest of the delectable treat into the fire. Their relationship lasted for a single autumn. When she called him eight months after they split up and asked to see him in person, he already knew what was coming, although he never would have guessed at his own reaction.

For their meeting, she chose a local coffee shop furnished with artfully mismatched tables, creaky chairs, and a collection of novelty candy dispensers arranged in colour-coordinated rows along the windowsill. The coffee came in cups that were more like bowls: smooth and round and thick. He ordered a black coffee, and she just had tap water.

Her baby bump looked strange on her thin body, as though it belonged to someone else.

"Is that a new shirt?" she asked, sipping her water, delicate as a hummingbird. They sat opposite one another in a booth by the window.

"I went to the mall the other day," he answered, though he was never entirely sure when she was making fun of him, because she had perpetually ironic eyebrows. "How are you?" he asked, feeling his heart floating up by his ears.

"It's a girl," she said, as if he were a stranger who had asked a different question. "It doesn't matter, though, does it?" Annie's mother glanced up and turned her head to stare either out the window or at the Daffy Duck PEZ dispenser on the sill, he couldn't be sure. "But, yeah. A girl." She was avoiding his gaze. "I just thought you should know that this happened," she said, gesturing at her own tummy. "Just, yeah. You know. It happened. But I've made the decision, so that part's done." She paused and sipped her water. "Anyway. They seem like they'll be good parents. They have a backyard. You don't need to do anything."

Jake wanted to turn his head so that he could see what she was looking at out the window, but he couldn't take his eyes off the bump. The only tenderness between them had always come from him, and there it was still, radiating out in bright beams, newly focused on her belly. As he sat there in the booth, watching her, he knew what he needed to do.

"I'll take her."

And that had been that.

Annie was skeptical about the camping gear at first. She hadn't been planning an outdoor adventure. Camping was something her friends sometimes did, it was true, but Annie avoided the Outdoor Education trips at school – which involved hiking, orienteering, and kayaking – and always opted instead for Mathletes. She had never even been much of a sleepover person because it freaked her out to be in unfamiliar houses at night. The first time she went to a slumber party, at age nine, she called her dad as soon as all the other girls fell asleep. As he drove them home that night, he told her he would come to get her whenever and wherever she needed, now and always. It was a promise she took so seriously that eventually he stopped going to bed at all when she was away, and sat by the phone instead, waiting for her inevitable call.

Although it had never really occurred to Annie that outdoor gear would be something she would ever need or want, it was better than the T-shirt with the photorealistic image of a hippo from the previous year. It was much better than the dangly earrings made out of miniature fish skeletons that he bought her for her eleventh birthday, and no one wants to bring up the extra-large puke-green fleece pajamas with the disconcerting flap over the backside that opened and closed with snaps. Her dad insists to this day that he hadn't noticed that part when he'd bought them, that he just thought they looked "cozy." Yes, compared to her dad's spectacularly poor selections over the years, the tent and camping gear seemed, well, inoffensive, and potentially even useful.

"Thank you," Annie said, and she meant it.

They hadn't always managed so perfectly, the two of them. Jake had never cooked vegetables "from scratch" before Annie started eating solid food, and when she was a toddler he had to pay a housekeeper to come over and teach him how to keep his own home clean enough for a little girl who put everything in her mouth. Fashion was not his strong suit: Annie showed up at her first day of preschool without underwear, which wouldn't have been as obvious if she had been wearing pants instead of a Snow White costume with a voluminous yellow skirt that flipped up when she went on the swings. And until one of the mothers pointed it out, he hadn't realized that skirts, unlike pants, usually zip up in the back rather than the front. He was secretly relieved when, at the age of five, Annie took charge of her own wardrobe, among other responsibilities. She was the one who, at ten, planted herbs in the window boxes and added throw cushions to the couch. At twelve, she took him to the department store to help him choose new small appliances for the kitchen when their blender grew so rickety it required a screwdriver to turn on. Annie and her father both figured, now, that they did okay, and that neither of them would want to change much about their little house on Alder Street.

It hadn't escaped Jake's attention that, like her mother, Annie had shown no real interest in camping up to this point. He didn't often compare her to her mother, since he hadn't, truthfully, known her mother all that well in the first place. He could identify only a few traits that might be genetically inherited – the way she walked, for example, making a shape like the letter A, with her arms held slightly further out from her body than was usual, and the particular auburn colour of her hair. Otherwise, Annie's self belonged just to Annie. This being the case, he hoped that camping could be given a fresh start for him, free of associations. Plus, with a tent so easy to work with and so light to carry, how could a person *not* want to go out and explore the big wide world?

"Will you look at that!" he kept saying. He circumnavigated the tent once more, careful not to knock over the neighbouring side table and magazine rack, and examined the parts until he began to worry that he had said it too many times, had got too into the details, and that his daughter's interest in her present was rapidly dwindling the more enthusiastic he became.

"Let's try it out," he said, trying not to sound overly eager. "Just to be sure it's good."

"Didn't we just do that?"

"To be sure it's good on the inside."

"Shouldn't we put the rain protector onto the outside first, like the instructions say?" Annie held up the single sheet and pointed to step number 3 of 3.

"Forecast for our living room says mostly sunny, but I suppose there's always the chance of rain."

"Dad." Annie raised one ironic eyebrow and tilted her head.

They slipped the rain cover over the tent and fastened it to each of the corners. When they finally crawled into the tent, they were surprised by how spacious it was inside. It was a three-man tent, and they were only two men, but it still seemed unexpectedly vast.

"We could get everyone we know in here, practically!"

"Yep. Come one, come all! Well, maybe everyone except Mrs. Mooney next door. She's put on a bit of weight lately."

"Dad! You're awful!"

"No, just being realistic about the capacity of our dwelling," Jake said, as he crawled out to grab the other wilderness supplies. They spread the sleeping bag out on the floor and opened the packet of freeze-dried ice cream, crunching the tiny shards of spumoni while they examined their surroundings.

"Will you look at that!" Jake said again, under his breath.

Annie was relieved that his present might actually work out. This time, she wouldn't be obliged to pretend to like her birthday gift, although her dad always knew immediately when she was faking. In past years, she had always waited at least twenty-four hours (a suitably polite amount of time) before asking for permission to mangle her present in some way for use in the "found objects" sculpture project with which Miss Bee, her art teacher, begins every year. Annie gets an A+ for found objects each time because Miss Bee has decided that these annual installments are, collectively, Annie's "conceptual autobiography." Apparently, they "comment on father-daughter relations in a postmodern consumer-driven world in which the gulf between self and other can never be bridged by material objects." Maybe this year, Annie thought, I won't get my A+.

"This is cool, Dad."

"Really?"

"Really. It feels like being inside a cathedral, almost, the way the ceiling is shaped."

"A waterproof worship-centre, assembled in less than five minutes," Jake said, adopting an infomercial voice as he held up his fist to his mouth like a microphone.

Annie lay down on the sleeping bag and looked up at the blue for the first time. As she tried to get space-worthy strawberry seeds out from between her teeth with her tongue, she felt, for a moment, as if the tent had become the whole world.

They hadn't meant for the tent to stay there. Jake was so excited that he had finally hit the mark, present-wise, that he hardly wanted to say anything when its continued presence in front of the pine bookcases and beside the living room set started to seem a bit odd. He knew he should probably exercise his parental authority at some point and insist that they tear down the camp; in truth, he didn't want to take it down any more than she did. Before the tent, Annie spent most of her time alone in her room. He never asked what she was doing, because he has not forgotten how much he hated his mother's constant nagging while he smoked pot in his bedroom when he was Annie's age. He was always curious, though, and wished that she would come down and watch TV with him. Back when her pajamas still had feet, she would beg to do just that, to stay up that extra half hour and fall asleep in his lap while he watched the news. Now she was the one who stayed up late, and he found himself wishing that he could curl up and fall asleep in the chair in the corner of her room while she talked to her friends on Gchat. If she'd wanted to come downstairs, he would have watched whatever she wanted to watch, even if it involved style makeovers or reality shows about spectacular desserts. Sometimes he walks up to the top of the stairs and stands outside her closed door, willing himself to knock, but he always goes back downstairs without asking her to join him. The idea of her saying no, however gently, is somehow worse than not asking at all. Besides, she was diligent about her homework, and although he worried about the fact that she didn't go out all that often or talk to him about her classmates, he knew she had friends at school. She went for a long run every other day and played field hockey, so really, how could he complain? She was basically the perfect kid, wasn't she?

In the weeks that followed the construction of the indoor campsite, two unexpected things happened: they began to spend their evenings together in the tent, and, to Jake's surprise, Annie began to open up to him. Like a seedling at first, offering gossip about the new music teacher at school, or her friend Miranda's constant battle with her sister over the use of their parents' car. Then, over the course of the first month of tent evenings, Annie burst into chatter as bright and full as a garden of prize-winning chrysanthemums. Her voice took on a new, sweet pitch when she told him about Todd, the shy math genius who sometimes stayed with her after class to work on bonus questions. "He's attentive, like he notices when I wear my hair up and stuff. And he's so smart, like he was explaining projective space to me, which is basically when . . ." Jake relished the warble of excitement when she explained hyperbolic geometry problems he wasn't sure he understood fully, even though he had learned the same things once himself. This was the first time she'd ever mentioned a boy, but Jake knew better than to say he was more interested in hearing about the boy than the math. He didn't want to slow the bloom of her banter. Instead, he watched Annie's face, relaxed and pointed up at the ceiling, bathed in the blue light. Then he closed his eyes and listened.

Six weeks after they put up the tent, Annie brought friends over after school to see it. As they walked to the house, the girls were suspicious.

"So, it's just a tent," said Miranda, checking her phone.

"Yep."

"Like, in your yard?" asked Juliana, who had wanted to go to the boys' soccer game.

"Nope," Annie replied.

"Where is it then?" asked Abi.

"You'll see," said Annie, fidgeting with her hair.

When the girls arrived in the living room, they remained unmoved.

"I don't get it," said Selisha, crossing her arms and looking at Juliana for support.

Juliana shifted her weight to one foot and stuck out her hip. "So, seriously," she said, "Kevin is playing goal today."

"Patience, grasshoppers," said Annie, opening the flap and sweeping her hand across the interior as though she were presenting the Taj Mahal. In the girls went, and for the first time since they left school, they stopped checking their phones. Miranda even brought her chewing to a standstill and let her gum harden between her teeth. At first, none of the girls said anything at all. They didn't quite know how to explain how it felt to be in the blue together. Annie sat in the middle, cross-legged, and closed her eyes. Her friends had never been so quiet. After a few minutes, they started giggling. Leslie snuggled into the corner and gave Krista a cuddle.

Miranda relaxed and blew a bubble. "It's awesome!"

"Thanks for having us, Annie," said Selisha.

Her father came home to find that there were eight girls inside the tent, and they didn't even seem squished, just happy and giggly and tinted a luminous blue.

"There's room for one more!"

"That's okay. Would you girls like a snack?"

"No food in the tent," said Annie.

"Except space food," her father countered.

"Not now, Dad." Annie closed the door flap, but not before giving her dad a wink.

After a couple of months, people in the neighbourhood started to ask questions. Mrs. Mooney noticed the tent through the living room window of the house next door when she and her husband were walking their dogs (she suspected hoarding), while the Jacksons, who drove past the plain brown house every day on their way home from work, wondered whether it was some kind of religious shrine. Some of the other neighbours started to ask one another if the tent had always been there and they'd just never noticed. No one knew Annie or her dad quite well enough to inquire.

It was the mailman who finally investigated one afternoon after working up the courage to do so for a very long time. For months, instead of delivering the mail to the box, he rang the doorbell every day. When Annie answered, he'd open his mouth as if to say something, but would pause for too long before holding the mail out to her and asking "Your mail?" It took Annie a few weeks to catch on that he was angling not just for an explanation but for an invitation.

"You've really got something here," he said after his first tent experience, hoisting his bag of letters back onto his shoulder.

"Don't I just?" said Annie, avoiding eye contact so as not to seem too proud.

The postman loved the tent so much that he brought his wife over the next day so that she could experience it too. It was a sensation. The postman told everyone he could about it, and in the days that followed, all of the neighbours came over to give it a try. Of course, Mrs. Mooney was the first to arrive.

"I hear you've got 'quite something' set up here," she said, miming air quotes with her fingers. "The postman won't tell me what it is, so I thought I'd come see for myself. I brought chocolate-caramel-coconut squares." She handed over a paper plate full of sticky confections and made a quick beeline for the tent.

"Well, thank you, Mrs. Mooney. Come on in," said Jake, shrugging at Annie as they followed behind her. When they peered in through the front flap, their busybody neighbour had plopped herself down in the very middle of the tent with her arms and legs crossed.

"So?" asked Annie.

"Well, I just never knew it could be so . . ." Mrs. Mooney spontaneously adopted a yoga pose, with both hands on her knees, palms facing up. "Actually, I would prefer to be left alone, if you wouldn't mind, so that I can have an authentic experience," she said, before zipping the front flap closed.

The day after Mrs. Mooney's visit, the Johnstones from #38 showed up on their doorstep with a fistful of freshly picked begonias from their garden, which they offered in exchange for some quality time in the tent. Even the neighbourhood curmudgeon, Drew Kendal, gave up on his reclusive habits and made the epic journey down the street on his walker, bearing chocolates filled with liquor. He spoke as if somewhere along the line he had been given lessons in elocution, and was always encouraging: "I've always thought exceedingly well of you, sir," the old man said, peering up at Jake from beneath his tufty eyebrows, "but now I feel quite confirmed in my supposition that you have been an excellent father and a true gentleman all these years. My sincerest commendation on this triumph." Mr. Kendal came back to the tent three more times and was not so cantankerous after all. Annie and her dad quickly found themselves surrounded by tokens of appreciation – bottles of wine, homemade pumpkin bread, and a frozen Quiche Lorraine – all within the first week. None of the neighbours had ever been inside their home before, so except for the fact that they had been living there for over a decade, it felt like a housewarming.

Much to Jake's surprise, the visitors did nothing but compliment him on the success of the birthday present and on raising such a fine young woman. He had expected somebody to comment on the unusual location of the tent, or at least to ask what was so special about putting an ordinary tent that anyone could buy at a department store in an ordinary living room that could be anyone's living room. Nobody reacted like that, though.

On the second Saturday that the tent was open to the public, Jake made lemonade and left a jug with Styrofoam cups by the door so that people could have a refreshing drink while they waited for their turn. By the end of the second weekend, they began to implement a system so that each visitor was guaranteed an equal amount of time in the tent. Jake was in charge of manning the door and restocking the refreshments, and Annie ran the egg timer, which made a clear, bright "ping!" when tent time was over.

Miss Bee, Annie's art teacher, started crying while she was in the tent. "It's simply astounding. A performance piece!" she said, hugging Annie afterwards. "I've never seen anything so sophisticated in my entire teaching career! The way you're involving the viewer in sensuous experience, Annie, and with no training in artistic practice."

"Hi, I'm Annie's dad," said Jake, sidling up to the two of them and extending his hand to the teacher.

"Your daughter has real talent," Miss Bee said, still clasping Jake's hand in both of hers. "I hope you realize how truly gifted she is."

"I didn't know I was being graded," Annie joked.

"Grades are hardly the point," said Miss Bee, finally releasing Jake's hand so she could wipe her eyes with a tissue. "But yes, A+."

By the fourth week, people began to drive from across town and gather in droves on the lawn to try out the tent. Because there could be quite a wait, Mrs. Jacobson, who worked at the Rec Centre, brought her face-painting supplies to keep the children entertained, and Mr. Reynolds set up a picnic blanket (complete with a romantic meal for him and his wife) on top of Annie's seedlings. There were even overly beloved pets waiting in line with their owners, including a ferret on a leash and a Labradoodle belonging to the Kinsey twins, who took turns holding onto her collar while the other twin went inside. Parking was a problem. Just as things were starting to get a bit chaotic (little Debbie Millhouse rode her tricycle off the front porch and two teenaged boys from Annie's class pummelled each other in the driveway), Mrs. Mooney took charge and shouted commands until everyone formed an orderly lineup. "Two by two!" she howled. "Johnny, I *see* you sneaking around the back . . ." The unruly crowd settled into a series of awkward pairings. Reverend Allott from St. Joseph's, still wearing his robes, made conversation about heavy garments in hot weather with his partner, Jonah the Goth, whose eye makeup was melting in the heat. Cindy Johnstone was allowed to take her teacup Yorkie as her partner, because she was too shy to go in with another human being.

Later that day, Annie got a phone call from the local newspaper asking if they could run a story. Annie was firm: "No reporters in the tent."

When September came and Annie went back to school, they could keep the tent open to the public only on the weekends. A tone of begrudging acceptance descended on the neighbourhood like a humid spell. They thought that was the end of it until Jake went outside to pick up the paper one morning and found an envelope taped to the door. It was a letter of complaint from the local seniors' centre, suggesting that to keep the tent open only on weekends was stressful and inconvenient for retirees and nurses who worked night shifts.

There were about thirty eager tent-goers gathered on the front lawn the morning Annie drew a sign in purple marker that said "CLOSED" – in what she hoped were friendly yet assertive bubble letters – and taped it to the door. Instead of letting the hype die down, Annie and her dad made the decision to close the tent at the peak of its fame, so that there was no let-down, no dwindling, just triumph. "With a bang, not a whimper," said Annie, reversing the T.S. Eliot line she'd been studying in English class. When she stepped aside to reveal the sign, the crowd erupted in disappointed jeers, and Annie apologized before closing and locking the door. "This is not what I was promised!" someone yelled from outside. People knocked on the door and pounded on the windows, shouting abuse and arguing with one another as they trampled what was left of Annie's front garden. As the day wore on, the would-be tent-goers began singing protest songs to the tuneful drone of Crafty Alex the kindergarten teacher's tissue-box guitar. "They'll be standing outside with banners next, protesting the injustices they've suffered," said Jake, and the two of them laughed so hard they had to hold each other by the elbows to stay upright.

"We don't need to worry, right?" Annie asked, still recovering from her fit of giggles.

"Of course not. They'll go away eventually," Jake replied, suddenly looking a little concerned.

After about six hours, as dusk began to settle around the bungalow and it became clear that the door would not open again, the crowd slowly started to disperse. A small group of unusually persistent stragglers sat on the doorstep for three more hours. Having exhausted their 1960s repertoire they had moved on to singing "The Wheels on the Bus Go Round and Round" over and over until it was well and truly dark, each protestor hoping that he or she would be the last one allowed inside.

The next morning, Annie and her dad got up early and, after checking that there was no one left on the lawn, they cleaned the tent carefully. They vacuumed the interior with a handheld DustBuster, aired out the sleeping bag, and even sprayed air freshener inside. They still had a dozen cans of frozen lemonade in their freezer and about four hundred Styrofoam cups. They were lemonaded out, but they figured they could encourage Mrs. Mooney's seven-year-old son to start a business. "I guess it was overkill on the cups," Jake said.

Back in the living room, they stood in front of the tent and thought again about taking it down, now that it had had its fifteen minutes. Annie leaned into her dad and he wrapped his arm around her.

"So, are there instructions for disassembly?" Jake asked.

"I don't think we even need them, do we?" Annie replied. "But I'm sure there's a sheet in the stuff-sac. Should we check?"

"Yeah," said Jake, without making a move towards the tent. "Okay."

"Are you ready?"

"How about we try it out one more time?"

"Sure, Dad," said Annie. "One last time just to make sure it's good inside."

Annie and her father closed the living-room curtains. They stood in front of the tent and gave each other a small nod before climbing in. Then they lay down side by side and settled into the blue.

THE COLLECTIVE NAME FOR NINJAS

☞ EVERY TIME THE NORTHERN LIGHTS WHISPER across the sky, Edward goes outside to listen. Since he moved north, it has been his retirement project to read all of the research on magnetic fields and auroral electrons, and now he knows all there is to know about them. Whether or not the lights make a real sound that is audible to the human ear is an open question, scientifically speaking, but Edward is sure he can hear a fizzling noise accompanied by a buzzing sensation that seems to course through his whole body. This is the empirical evidence on which he bases his conclusions, but the sound is something more, too. It's sparklers lighting up in his blood, flashing from his fingers up to his earlobes, and radio waves inside his eyelids. Nothing else has ever made Edward feel the way he does when he's standing under the big green sky – like he's at the very centre of the hum, as if the curve of his inner ear contains the whole known universe, spiral galaxies bouncing off his eardrums. But surely even his ecstasy can be explained. When he finds a way of measuring vibrations to prove that we can really hear the lights, that there may even be a stimulation that causes synesthesia, he will publish it to great acclaim in *Science*. It will be his last article: his swan song.

It remains a great disappointment for Edward that his daughter, Jess, has never been sufficiently impressed by natural phenomena. "I know, Dad, they're nice," she says, checking her grocery list on her iPhone as he tells her about his discoveries. "I can't hear anything, personally, but if you want to measure the waves, you should."

Nice. How could she possibly describe the lights that way? Even though she means to be reassuring, they are simply not "nice" any more than fetal pig dissection is "nice." Edward is sure that his eleven-year-old grandson, Sam, will feel differently than his mother does. Unfortunately, the sky only opens up at night, when Sam is in bed. Because of Jess's lack of interest and the strict sleeping regimen she keeps for her son, she never wakes Sam up to take him outside to see the spectacle. Even when Edward calls her in the evening to suggest it, he knows she never takes her son out into the night air to eavesdrop. Before he can even begin to explain that Sam, with all the intensity of his youth, will surely feel the experience to the fullest, an exasperated breath usually emerges from the receiver in response. Sometimes, he thinks her reedy breathing is her best effort to be kind, that she'd rather make a noise like static on the line than say anything to upset him. During these conversations, Edward often holds the telephone away from his ear and stares at it, as if it is the phone and not his daughter sighing at him before wishing him a good sleep.

Some evenings, now that it's getting dark earlier, Edward drives two-and-a-half hours out of town to a place where he can be alone with the sky. He unfolds a camping chair on the gravel by the side of the road, the wide yawn of canola fields beside him, and just listens with his whole self.

Sam takes his own hobbies seriously. His latest obsession is with ancient Japanese combat. This is why Edward owns a ninja outfit of the finest quality that Sam helped him to purchase online – a clean and unworn set of black clothes, including slim jacket, ballooning trousers, balaclava, as well as a set of ninja stars, nunchuks, and, of course, a long sword in a black leather sheath that slips into the suit's belt. The sword is astonishingly heavy and Edward needs both hands to carry it. His only regular form of exercise, now that his cycling days are over, is repeatedly grasping a spring-loaded device designed to develop his grip, so although he has forearms of steel, his general upper body strength leaves something to be desired. Never mind. Edward has no practical experience with ninjas aside from what his grandson has taught him, but if he wanted to, he could really look the part. The getup has to be hidden away so that Sam's mother doesn't find the sword and scold Edward for condoning violence and for spoiling her son by indulging his fantasies. According to the floor plans that Sam has drawn up, the kitchen is the heart-centre of Edward's house, readily reachable at any moment. Edward has stored the ninja collection carefully, so that the outer curve of the weapon just touches the upper cabinet door without scratching.

Edward and Sam have lunch together every day, since Sam's school is across the street. Despite having lived alone since his wife, Wendy, died thirteen years ago, Edward is still not quite accustomed to cooking for only one person. He often instinctively makes two sandwiches, or measures milk into two cups, even if he ends up pouring tea over only one of them. He suspects this means he is getting old. Jess has threatened to abandon him to the care of the elderly ladies who swim at the community rec centre should he ever become senile, so he never confesses his culinary misjudgments to her. He assumes she's joking about the old dears, but the idea still fills Edward with a feeling of authentic dread. He simply cannot abide the notion of himself standing poolside in a speedo, swimcap, and goggles, soggy and wrinkled as a Shar-Pei puppy. This is not everyone's idea of torture, and Edward knows that Jess means well with her mockery, but he finds it simply impossible to think of anything more humiliating than Seniors' Aquafit at the public swimming pool. At any rate, Sam puts him right at lunchtime. They eat grilled cheese sandwiches and share a can of SpaghettiOs or Campbell's Tomato Soup, slurping from teaspoons as they watch crime dramas and worry inwardly.

In a way, it's a shame Sam has to go to school at all. Edward had taught his grandson how to read by the time he was four years old, and, a year later, to write, although early literacy was their secret. Even when he was in diapers, Sam would ignore the other children at preschool and sit on the carpet, silent and regal as a king, books piled high around him like a fortress. Edward knew that although Sam seemed a toddler of few words, he was, in fact, a miniature master of acrostics, turning the letters over and around in his mind until they fit just so. Despite Edward's assurances, Sam's parents and teachers grew concerned when he remained silent in the classroom throughout grade one, preferring to sit on the floor and pull book after book off the shelf just to look – or so the teacher thought – at the pictures. It wasn't until just after he turned seven, after many visits to the school counsellor, several aptitude tests, and countless fits of parental anxiety, that Sam announced his reading to his grade two teacher by finishing a full-length spy novel in French, about which he wrote, in perfect cursive, a book review.

Today the two of them are sitting at the folding card table that Edward keeps in the living room for when Sam comes over, so that they can eat and watch TV at the same time. He used to fold the table away and then put it out again every day, but he has recently taken to just leaving it beside the couch across from the TV, slightly crowding the space, but saving his back for more important challenges. When *Law and Order* comes on, Sam and Edward chime in, "In the criminal justice system, the people are represented by two separate, yet equally important groups: the police, who investigate crime, and the district attorneys who prosecute the offenders. These are their stories." Sam punctuates this last line by pounding his fists gleefully on the table. Edward considers telling him to be more careful, as Sam's soup wobbles near the edge of his bowl, but instead he stands, and asks if he'd like anything else.

"No, Granddad. There's a robbery taking place."

In the kitchen, Edward puts on the kettle and opens the cupboard to admire the ninja gear. Funny to have acquired so much apparel when what most appeals to him is the ninja's ability to become entirely invisible. This is his aspiration: to be everywhere and be seen nowhere; to get in no one's way, and yet still be able to stand up for oneself, if this were called for. Perhaps being old is its own kind of stealth, but Edward would like to be more glamorously invisible. Of course, it is not the ninja's cunning or transparency that most attracts Sam. For him the glory is all in the image. The ripple of black harem pants in the wind as the creature flies from a rooftop and lands silently on padded feet. The mask. The sword. Sam's right; it is an appealing uniform. Edward pours himself a mug of tea and carries out a small china cupful with extra sugar to Sam. They settle into a gritty alleyway, where an unhelpful shopkeeper is leading investigators astray.

Edward lived in Vancouver for nearly seventy years before moving to northern British Columbia to be near Jess and her family when he retired two years ago. Real estate here costs nothing compared to the city, so when he moved, the contents of his small, tidy apartment seemed to spill out across the three-bedroom, two-storey house like a riot of prizes from a piñata. Sam has his own bedroom upstairs, and Edward uses the other spare room as his library. Set against one wall is a bookshelf with all of his own publications and notes, the bound doctoral theses of his former students, and several now-outdated reference books that once thought they could explain global warming. His degrees are somewhere in a box. On the opposite wall is a roll-top desk equipped with a brown leather desk set. His mother's copy of *The Complete Works of Robert Burns* takes pride of place on the desk's built-in shelf, and Edward keeps two letter openers and one blue ballpoint in the pen cup. On the desk are several of Sam's drawings, all of which depict empty rooms. The first time Sam presented

Edward with a pencil-drawn picture of a classroom full of vacant desks, Edward had been confused.

"Don't you get it?" Sam had asked, impatient.

Edward looked harder, then shook his head.

"A room full of ninjas!" Sam exclaimed, crouching down on the floor and raising an imaginary sword.

Edward let out his loud, gulping laugh, so Sam, encouraged, had gone on to sketch every room he knew and fill them with invisible martial artists. This made Sam quite skilled at representing furniture. For a while, Edward kept the ninja clothing locked inside the closed desk along with the drawings, but he knew that Jess had a key, and that in the event of his unexpected demise, it was the first place she would look for his Last Will and Testament. He isn't entirely sure, actually, what Jess would think of the ninja obsession, but he suspects that it would go against the strict anti-violence policy that his daughter and her husband uphold. He could picture her now, pedantically explaining the "Little Bang" parenting theory, which suggests that the use of toy guns by small boys leads to a higher incidence of violent crime in the teenage years. It pains him that Jess would be so gullible despite the fact that she had been such an exceptional student when she was younger. The theory, at least as Jess describes it, relies on a basic logical fallacy that confuses correlation with causation. To make matters worse, the newspaper article she showed him clearly indicated that the study on which the theory was based had relied on twenty volunteers: hardly a large or diverse enough group of participants to produce generalizable results. If she had gone to university and followed through on her early intellectual promise, she could have been a much better researcher than these parenting-theory frauds. And anyway, Edward has enough confidence in his grandson to be quite sure Sam won't whip out the nunchuks on the playground. Still, he is convinced that it would be better for everyone if Sam could commandeer the ninja gear before his mother finds it.

Sam sips his sweet tea without unfixing his eyes from the scene on the TV of a man dressed in a woman's wig and sporting voluptuous red lips being interviewed by a po-faced attorney. Edward has been paying less attention. He checks his watch and comes to the conclusion that this episode will be continued tomorrow. Sam tips the sugar from the bottom of his teacup into his mouth before turning to face Edward as the closing credits begin to roll.

Edward clears the bowls, and when he returns from the kitchen, Sam is sitting on the couch, tilting his head to read Edward's notes in the margins of the heavily annotated *Aurora Watcher's Handbook* that he must have left on the coffee table. It is unlike Edward to leave his books scattered around the house, and even less like him to have drafts or scribbles out in the open like this; but instead of feeling protective of his unfinished work, he can't help but feel that Sam ought to be reading the notes. Somehow, perhaps even without realizing it, he had written in the margins not for himself but for his grandson.

Sam's hair has blonded in the sun, and his jean shorts are becoming a bit too little for his lengthening legs. As his grandson shifts slightly on the couch, Edward sees a scrape on one of

Sam's small knees and feels a fondness open up in his chest like a golf umbrella. He wants nothing more than to have Sam reclining on a lawn chair beside him under the night sky, listening to the hum and feeling as though he's holding thunder between his teeth. Edward is tired of arguing with Jess about taking Sam out with him. Whatever Jess might say, Sam simply needs to hear the lights at their best. He's tried to get Sam to sneak out of bed without his mother's permission, has offered to lend him a hand-held sound level meter to hide under his pillow, but Sam is a heavy sleeper and an obedient son. Time, Edward decides, to take matters into his own hands.

"Sam, I was thinking."

"What?"

"I'm going to take you back to school, and when you've finished, I'll have a surprise ready. Will I meet you at the crossing guard at three, or is today soccer day?"

"Soccer," says Sam, without taking his eyes off the book.

"Right. Well. Four-thirty then. In the parking lot."

After he's walked Sam back to school and picked up some milk and bananas at the corner store, Edward paces excitedly around his house. He hopes the sky will be ready for them. To distract himself, Edward begins to clean. He scrubs down the card table, and vacuums the living room rug. He dusts the bookshelves and the TV, polishes the glass on the coffee table, and only when the last of his wife's milk-glass candy dishes on the side table has been dusted and refilled does he sit down on the couch. He turns on the radio and listens to someone playing an amateurish rendition of "There Will Never Be Another You" on the saxophone. The saxophonist is, as Edward guessed, a high-school music student auditioning for the Youth Jazz Orchestra. Edward is momentarily proud of her. These kinds of accomplishments are worth appreciating. He had been so pleased when his own children took piano lessons, and so disheartened when, one by one, all three stopped once they reached the age of fourteen. When Jess first started her piano lessons, Edward decided to take a few classes himself. It didn't last long. He couldn't bring himself to endure his plodding fingering as he fumbled through Bach's easier Preludes. Although he would never have said so, he was also ashamed to be outdone by his then five-year-old daughter. Jess had always been the most promising of his children.

Edward goes over the familiar route to his favourite roadside spot in his head, and checks the provisions in the car to make sure everything is in order: he has a map (just in case), his own field notes and a fresh notebook for Sam, a sound level meter, a video camera, two flashlights, and three freshly sharpened pencils. He has had an extra lawn chair in the trunk of his car since he started his expeditions. Edward has always been the sort of person to carry multiples of his supplies, but he would be lying if he said that this was just a spare. He makes a peanut butter and banana sandwich for Sam, and zips it into a zip-lock bag, sucking the air out with a straw to keep the bread from going stale. He phones his daughter and leaves her a message, making up some excuse for her about an early-morning soccer practice and explaining that he's happy to have Sam stay the night if she and Kevin want some time to themselves. He packs his ninja gear into the trunk of his car and then settles himself into the driver's seat, tapping his fingers against the steering wheel as he waits for the minutes to pass. Finally, it is time to get Sam.

Edward knows it is ridiculous to drive the short distance to the school, but he doesn't want them to go home first, where they would be likely to settle into the couch and choose coziness over adventure. He is always early when he picks up Sam, but today he has a full twenty minutes to kill. He checks his tires and then leans back against the car and watches the soccer team practise throw-ins, the balls flying in neat parabolas over the field. Eventually, Sam comes barrelling along the gravel path and into the parking lot and wraps his arms around Edward's belly. Once they're inside the car, Sam makes his usual request as he does up his seatbelt.

"Snack?"

"This is your first mission," Edward replies. "The snack is in the car, and it is your task to find it."

Sam giggles. He looks at his granddad and rolls the window up and down, pretending to search outside.

"I don't see it."

"Not much of an effort."

Sam sticks out his tongue slightly to the side in concentration, suddenly concerned about the strange challenge, when he's so used to being immediately handed a treat. He has inherited his grandfather's worrywart tendencies, which seem to have skipped a generation. When Sam opens the glove compartment, he finds a sandwich, a map, and a ninja star inside. He grabs the snack and stares earnestly at his grandfather.

"Where are we going?"

"It's a surprise!" Edward says, and then pauses to reconsider how much he should tell Sam. "But first we have to stop for gas."

As they pull up to the gas station, Edward suspects it would be best if he called his daughter to make sure she received his earlier message. He doesn't want her to be suspicious about the change to their daily arrangement. Jess usually stops by Edward's house after work to collect Sam, though she seldom comes inside. Sam is never quite ready to go home. As he gathers his things and slowly ties his shoelaces – making one side of the bow and then the other, and then starting again to make the loops more even – Edward and Jess stand on the porch and chat for a few minutes about her work at the gallery or her Sunday art classes. Despite his warnings, Jess had somehow failed to realize that her artistic skill would never earn her a proper wage – that no matter how inventive her sculptures, how careful her drawings, it was never quite enough. For a while she juggled three jobs while taking care of Sam and barely made anything beautiful at all, until finally Kevin had told her that they would still manage if she cut back on work. Edward had moved by then, hoping that he would be able to help by taking care of Sam after school. But her small complaints about the community centre have accumulated in the past five years, and so their porch conversations are nearly always vocational. Lately, he has noticed a tiredness in her face that never used to be there, and a small red vein just below her eye has burst, like a beauty mark gone wrong.

She tries on new job ideas for him like outfits. When she told him her latest idea of going back to school to train as a chef, Edward tried to catch himself, to think of what Wendy would have said, but instead he blurted out, "Hard life. Terrible hours." He has always been the first to point out the drawbacks in someone else's plan.

"I suppose you're right. It wouldn't be the best thing for Sam. I just wish I had thought it all through a bit more, you know, longer term. I knew that the sculpture course was right at the time. It wasn't even a question. Now, I'm just not so sure about it, you know? Like maybe it *was* wrong and now it's too late to switch up my whole plan."

"Well, I'm not the right person to ask." Edward couldn't help but feel that he'd told her so: that if she'd done what he'd wanted her to at the time and taken chemistry at university, they wouldn't be having this conversation.

"No. No, you're not." She touched him lightly on the arm as she spoke and Edward interpreted this as a gesture of affection. As soon as Sam was all set, Jess rushed him into the car, leaving her aspirations at Edward's door, and reversed out of the driveway without waving.

At the gas station, Edward hands Sam a dollar for candy and sends him into the convenience store while he waits outside beside the phone booth. Edward picks up the receiver and tries to remain calm as he dials her number. Of course Jess is happy for Sam to sleep over, and Edward is amazed by the brightness of his own voice as he reassures her that the two of them are getting along famously. "Great! We'll see you tomorrow after school, then!" His hands are strong and unwavering too, wrapped around the base of the phone. Perhaps he is cut out for this kind of escapade after all.

Sam returns with two licorice sticks and some fuzzy peaches. Only then does Edward notice that he's still wearing his soccer shoes and hasn't brought a jacket. After spending a whole afternoon preparing for their trip, he can't believe he still managed to forget Sam's green windbreaker, which is hanging on a hook by the back door at home. Well, there's a rain slicker of his own in the back that Sam can borrow if the March air gets chilly. They climb back into the Toyota. Not the most ninja-appropriate vehicle, Edward decides, momentarily regretting the pine-scented cardboard tree hanging from the rear-view mirror. But, then, Edward himself is still wearing an argyle sweater-vest, so even the Batmobile or James Bond's Aston Martin would have done little to counteract the quaint exterior of their research expedition. Ninjas have many enviable skills, but peer-reviewed articles are not, Edward supposes, their usual contributions to culture. Perhaps the Toyota is for the best.

Edward has not been shopping for clothes since Wendy died. Actually, he is wearing the last pair of trousers she bought for him the year before she went to the care facility and, eventually, to hospice. Jess has tried to buy him a shirt or two for Christmas, but it was no use. He has to become accustomed to his clothes before he can really wear them, and the shirts that Jess bought him came in horrible patterns and were not very soft. Before his retirement he had managed to buy a few new ties, at least, thinking that these would spruce up his teaching wear and that strips of coloured fabric would be difficult to get wrong.

Wendy used to choose his suits, trousers, and shirts for him by rubbing the fabric between her thumb and index finger, then holding them up against him and offering him two choices so that Edward would feel that he had picked the clothes himself. There was never any dithering and she had a good eye. She had done this for him since they got married, when his mother had stopped buying his clothes. It is strange, he often thinks, the skills one doesn't acquire when one is taken care of, and how difficult new things can be to learn.

As they begin to drive past the single row of shops on the main drag, Edward can tell that Sam is uneasy about being on this road trip instead of at home in front of cartoons. Sam doesn't say anything, but he begins to stretch his neck as he gazes intently out the window, as if he's keeping track of each detail in case he never sees it again. Then, he begins to tap out a rhythm on his knees with his fingers. To keep his grandson occupied, and to ease his own anxieties about having lied to Jess, Edward poses a complicated question. "What do you suppose is the collective term for ninjas?"

"Collective . . . ?" Sam looks quizzical for a moment. "Oh, like the poster in my room. A murder of crows, a bellowing of bullfinches, an ostertation of peacocks?"

"Ostentation of peacocks. But yes, that's what I mean. Ninjas?"

Sam and Edward ponder the possibilities. Edward loves the educational poster he bought for Sam. It depicts groups of animals acting out their collective nouns, so there are crows wielding bloody knives and aristocratic peacocks preening in front of a gilt-rimmed mirror. Sam generally prefers the World Flags poster, but he has nevertheless memorized the names for each animal group.

"*Swarm*?" Edward suggests.

Sam is unimpressed. "That's taken. Bees come in swarms." He pauses. "How about a *surprise*?"

Edward imagines enormous cartoon eyes peeking out through a ninja mask. "A surprise of ninjas. That will do."

Sam seems to be contemplating his own genius by biting his bottom lip.

They are both beginning to relax as they pull out onto a stretch of road that leads to miles and miles of farmland. The rounded hay bales seem to fall behind them like Hansel and Gretel's crumbs dotting the path home. Edward loves the prairies. They could drive for hours and not see another person. On the radio, a lexicographer talks about the introduction of the word *crunk* to the dictionary. It's not long before Sam's head is cradled in the shoulder strap of his seatbelt and his eyes are closed, his mouth slightly open. Riding in the passenger seat beside Edward always makes Sam sleepy. Jess had been the same way. When she was ten, Jess heard that a schoolmate's grandmother had "died in her sleep," and so she had refused to go to bed, because she worried every night that she was closing her eyes for the last time. For weeks after, Edward drove her all over North Vancouver after dark because it was the only way to get her to sleep. Sometimes he wishes he could still do that – drive until she closed her eyes, until he was sure it was a deep slumber, and then head home, open the car door carefully, and gather her up in his arms. Sam looks just the way Jess did sleeping in the car, lips parted as if he's about to say something and every so often letting out a quiet almost-snore. Edward keeps both hands on the wheel. How much longer will the ninja phase last? he wonders. How long until the ninja stars and nunchuks are not just hidden away but forgotten? How long until Sam's secrets remain his alone?

Edward tries to concentrate on the road. An old cassette that Jess gave him when she upgraded to CDs is in the tape deck of the car, so he pushes play and turns it down to a low volume, careful not to wake Sam. It's Crosby, Stills, and Nash: his daughter's driving track of choice. This reminds him of the moral grey area he's currently occupying, having misled Jess about the reason for the sleepover, so he quickly turns the tape off again. Edward has never been an impulsive man, nor has he ever been a brave one. He tries to imagine how he would describe himself, but all he can think of are negatives – the kind of person he is not. Not charismatic. Not outgoing. Not cherished, not truly, or at least not anymore. He lets out a slow breath.

They pass three separate prairie towns and several gas stations, and finally, at seven p.m. Edward pulls over. The lights will be more spectacular in an hour or two, but he likes to arrive at his chosen spot early to hear them grow louder as the sky darkens. He gets out of the car to stretch his legs. He paces along the ditch by the side of the road and unzips his pants to pee into it. He walks back to the car and looks through the window at Sam, who is now curled up in the seat with his feet tucked up underneath him. He understands now why Jess wouldn't want to wake him. Eventually, Edward opens the trunk and removes the ninja clothes. He unfolds them carefully, then opens the passenger-side door and lays the heroic outfit over Sam, tucking his grandson in. Edward opens the trunk again and gets out his notebook and his frequency meter. Then he sets up his lawn chair in his usual spot by the side of the road, and prepares himself to listen, as always, alone.

EACH SMALL THING

WELL, HELLO THERE! YOU'RE JUST IN TIME TO join us. Don't be shy, there's plenty of room on the tour. I was just about to say that the world was never small in the way that Jemima Hendricks wanted it to be. No matter how long she spent super-gluing exquisite bows onto miniature hairlines, or embroidering tea towels the size of hamsters' toes, there was no potion that could make the world shrink, Alice-in-Wonderland style, to the size she had in mind. Still, you wouldn't think that figurines no more than a third of an inch tall could ever take up much space, but even the smallest things become clutter when there are too many of them.

That's my interpretation, anyway, of how the Hendricks Memorial Miniatures Museum came to be. My name is Amy and I'll be taking you through Miniatureland today. That's what we call it around here because the whole memorial thing is such a mouthful. I hope you'll feel cordially welcomed at our establishment, which has been voted the top tourist attraction here in Dithers for five years running by *Tip Top Tourists* magazine. That's a province-wide publication, so the award is truly an honour.

As your guide, I feel it's important that you all get to know

Jemima. A lot of tourists come through here without ever learning a thing. Those are the people who make the regrettable decision to decline this tour – or to go with one of the less qualified guides here, but don't tell anyone else I said that. I don't mean to be catty but honestly, you met Cody at the front desk on your way in, right? Just look at him out there now: standing by the door, smoking a substance that I suspect from the particular cock of his wrist is not a cigarette. Paragon of emotional maturity, he is not! I hope you weren't turned off by that first impression. But I shouldn't be so hard on him: I wouldn't choose to be a teenager again for all the money in the world, would you?

Our wander through the wonderful world of the tiny will take about sixty minutes, but you can stay afterwards and look around all day if you want. The ticket price includes unlimited entry. The tour shunners don't take advantage of the full-day policy. No, they prefer to breeze by the fairy-tale castles and the battleships and the model railway, pose like amateur catalogue models in front of the mini Colosseum, and take pictures with flash. Some holiday-makers are in and out in less than half an hour. Refusing the tour strikes me as especially rude since the gorgeous specimen of Arts and Crafts architecture in which you now stand used to be Jemima's home. So, I appreciate the time that you are taking with me today. You three are going to get the best experience that this place can offer.

Jemima was born in 1932 and started her work in miniatures when she was nine years old. The first of her models was a gift from an English uncle who claimed to be called Barnaby Supple, though everyone knew that this wasn't a family name. She met him only once, when he showed up unannounced at the door of her family's home in the summer of 1941. He likely declared his presence using the original feature you no doubt noticed on your way in, the brass monkey's head knocker. Although Mr. Hendricks had not seen his older brother since before Jemima was born, I like to imagine that he opened the door slowly and shot a worried look at his wife, as if Barnaby might try to sell them an afterlife they didn't want.

Barnaby was a barber by trade, which anyone could see by observing his own luxuriant waxed mustache. Years later in her diaries, Jemima reflected on that day and wrote that she had never met anyone like him – and certainly no one who seemed to have thought more about the appearance than the function of his clothes, or who had a sense of style beyond the necessities of day-to-day life. She could not stop staring at his striped trousers and his tweed waistcoat with its flat ivory buttons that sat smooth even over his rotund tummy. He looked like a sea-bedraggled walrus in its Sunday best, bringing the whole ocean in with him. Jemima's mother scolded her for staring, and sent her to fetch the tea, which Jemima made and carried back to the living room as quickly as she could. Once he'd settled in and the tea was steeping on a tray beside him, Barnaby knelt down on the floor beside Jemima and shook her hand with the same level of formality he had offered her parents. Then, he reached into his battered suitcase and handed Jemima a Make-Your-Own Victorian Dollhouse kit. On the box was an illustration of a girl prettier and sweeter and blonder than Jemima, holding up a giant pair of craft scissors.

Along with the dollhouse, Barnaby gave Jemima bangs that made her face look as round as a dinner plate. Her new ragged haircut accentuated the worry lines she had already developed on her forehead, and she tried unsuccessfully to blow them out of the way when she sat with the grown-ups at dinner. The wrinkles deepened when she opened the box carefully and started to lay out the pieces of her first project on the floor. This very floor, in fact, where we stand now, though at that time there was an ornate floral-printed area rug. She wanted to unpack the toy in just the right way, and was nervous about disappointing Barnaby, who sat close by, waiting expectantly for her reaction to the present. The people in the kit were two-dimensional figures cut in perforated lines and all she had to do was pop the shapes out of thin wooden sheets as you would with a paper doll. The house had clear instructions: slot A fits into B, then C into D, then on go the two pieces of the roof and there you have it! A bungalow! The house came together so quickly and looked so professional that for a moment Jemima could almost imagine that she was not herself after all, but was the girl on the box: all ribbon and satin and handmade glory.

Uncle Barnaby helped with the kit by galumphing onto the floor, settling on the carpet beside her, and holding the house still as well as his trembling hands would allow him while Jemima daubed glue onto the chimney. (Apparently, he also played with the dolls and made them kiss each other, which scandalized Jemima, who even in her youth preferred construction to play-acting.) No adult before Barnaby had ever knelt on the floor with Jemima and made knowing eye contact with her, as if she too were grown up. Her parents, for instance, preferred the safe distance of the sofa, where they existed slightly above Jemima, in a private world of anxious murmurs about fish and finance. In fact, Jemima imagined growing up as a process of ascending – floating up from the carpet to the couch.

When the dollhouse was assembled, Barnaby praised it lavishly. He lifted Jemima's arms up in victory as if she'd won a wrestling match, and she felt, for the first time, like she'd accomplished more than she'd set out to do. Unfortunately, Barnaby was unable to assist Jemima with any more of her projects, since he left as abruptly as he arrived, a matter of days after he first appeared at their door. He departed in such a rush that he left behind a trail of stray objects: a book of the seven wonders of the ancient world, into which he had pasted photographs and written notes from his own travels, a flask half full of pungent liquor, and a single, size twelve, black-and-white wingtip shoe. As you'll see upstairs, the seven wonders book provided the inspiration for at least, well, seven of the dioramas we exhibit. Barnaby's dollhouse will be the last item we'll see on this floor before we head upstairs. It's displayed alongside the book, the flask, and the shoe.

Even with this earliest model, Jemima went beyond the kit's instructions. The parts provided were delightful, but after Barnaby's departure she couldn't help but feel that there was more work to do. She added to the house gradually over the following three years, constructing a bathtub, for instance, out of an old sardine can and papering the walls in layers of bright candy wrappers. She painted expressive faces on the dolls and clothed them in printed dresses and tailored suits made out of scraps from her mother's sewing basket. In her early teenage years, Jemima began to add extensions to the house, including a cellophane greenhouse containing a single bird of paradise fashioned in origami from a postage stamp.

Needless to say, Jemima's juvenilia were steps towards a more refined version of her craft. After Barnaby's dollhouse came miniatures of each of the seven wonders in succession. At first she relied on mail-order catalogues for pre-made dolls and tiny rolltop desks and stove-top kettles. These she combined with more inventive furnishings of her own construction made from seashells, beach glass, and elastic bands.

You'll notice as we work our way through the exhibits that over her career as a miniaturist, Jemima's creations became smaller and smaller. By 1988 she was working with a laboratory-quality microscope and using implements designed for the dissection of insect wings. The smallest artifacts you'll see in the museum are in this display to our right, which has been set up with microscopes so that you can appreciate the intricacy of these late works. If you take a peek – yes, don't be shy! Have a good look! – you'll see a lighthouse made out of a grain of rice. Then, next to it in the display case are four balsa-wood elephants and a plastic elephant trainer inside the eye of a needle. Finally, you have a summer cottage that's no larger than a crystal of sea salt. By the time she was working at this minute scale, it took Jemima six months to produce one figurine. The cottage, for example, consists of 107 individual polymer clay pieces, which are completely invisible to the naked eye. Legend has it that she spent a year and a half rendering the shell of an oyster, complete with a single pearl, only to have it vanish when she sneezed.

I'd like us to pause by the second display here. Why don't you find a spot with a good view? This magnificent house, which you'll see is larger than most of the miniatures in the museum, has six rooms and measures exactly two feet tall from the tip of the roof to the foundations. In order to fully appreciate the craftsmanship, I'd like to take you through each room. To offer you a tour within the tour, so to speak, and make sure that you appreciate the key details that set these models apart from your average child's plaything.

I always begin with this particular building because it's my favourite. It's not the most lavish – that would have to be the Taj Mahal – nor is it the most complicated – the English country manor to our right might take that title on account of the fully functional watermill. The museum is not organized chronologically. We've gone for a thematic approach: dollhouses and domestic spaces here on the ground floor, natural and man-made wonders upstairs, and in the attic is outer space and the ocean. Other tour guides might organize the visit differently, starting with the European castles montage or the moon landing with all of its black-lit stars, but sometimes the most important details are the ones people overlook when they rush through. I prefer to draw your attention down to the level of a mole painted on a doll's cheek or to a shrub that conforms to accurate botanical descriptions. As you can see, Jemima could glitz it up with the best of the artisans, but her own taste tended more towards the small moments one might instinctively forget. Besides, I like to think that half an hour per tour is a loose time guideline, not a hard and fast rule.

At the top of the house is the attic, which hides in the peak of the pointed roof. No one lives there, but it's not an attic stuffed with heirlooms that might one day be uncovered. There are no trunks full of letters or black-and-white photographs, but there is speculation in the scholarly community that Jemima may at one point have constructed the trunks and then removed them. Professor Norbridge, an expert from the University of British Columbia in the history of early twentieth-century domestic hobbies, visited the museum in 2010 and showed us some historical reconstructions of an early version of the room. Or, as much as the academics can recreate it from descriptions in Jemima's personal papers, anyway. But let me just say *I* had a lot to teach *him*, which was a real treat for me since he's an actual expert.

As I'm sure you can see, the walls are constructed to look incomplete, with exposed beams fashioned from whittled, walnut-stained unsharpened pencils and pink insulation made of hand-dyed cotton wool. Note the single bare light bulb. If you look closely, you'll see that instead of a light switch, there's a string hanging from the ceiling just behind the bulb. If you pull it, delicately, using only your thumb and index finger, the bulb wakes up, even now, like a sleepy glow-worm, and the string dances as it catches the new light. No, ma'am, you can't pull it. As you can see, the entire house is behind glass, being kept safe in the cabinet. Even I have turned the light on only once by hand, as a reward for being Miniatureland's most committed tour guide in 2007. I also received a complimentary spa visit for two at The Oasis. I took the runner-up tour guide, Jenna, because that's how much of a team player I am.

The electricity in the house works, by the way. Every filament of every bulb can produce a little glimmer of light. See that green button on the wall to the left of the display case? If you'd like to press that, sir, you'll see all the lights of the house come on. Yes! There we go. Don't worry, it's not witchcraft. I'll explain the masterful engineering later. On the attic floor is a trap door with a matchstick ladder that folds down, but no one ever uses it on account of how tiny the crawl space is, and also because all the inhabitants of the house are rather restricted in the mobility department. They are confined to their rooms, each glued into a single daily activity for all eternity. Even the houseguests never leave. They also never overstay their welcome.

The Hendricks were a church-going family. Mr. Hendricks worked for thirty-eight years in the local fish cannery. Jemima wrote that his beard smelled like the inside of a mussel shell and his hands were the colour of sockeye salmon. Mrs. Hendricks made her famous Bakewell tarts for every church bake sale and did some bookkeeping for the cannery when the usual girl was on holiday. Jemima was their only child. Mrs. Hendricks suffered four miscarriages before her daughter was born, and two more afterwards. We know all this because she kept a diary. The forty-seven volumes are housed next door in the same building as the oldest, largest, and most wonderful cabinet of curiosities in British Columbia. I'm supposed to tell you that you should check that out after your visit with us. The diaries are still restricted-access files, because of their age and fragility, but I was lucky enough to receive permission to enter the archive last summer.

I'm sad to say that reading Mrs. Hendricks's diaries was not an altogether scintillating experience. In fact, I think I'd better stop calling them "diaries" so no one gets too excited about them. When I sat down at the desk in the archive and opened my first little navy leather book, I found that Mrs. Hendricks's daily records were in fact ledgers, and contained point-form lists of what she cooked each day, who came calling from her church group, the entire family's medical history, and a record of every penny she spent. No, sorry, I don't know how the currency would convert based on inflation, so I can't tell you what the numbers mean, but I don't get the impression that she was a big spender. The cabinet of curiosities attracts more visitors, because of the preserved bull testicles and the camera obscura, but I know when I'm in there with those leather books that I am the beholder of historically significant, if outwardly tedious treasures. Anyway, it's a good thing we have the notebooks, because they tell us, through the indisputable logic of cake recipes, that Jemima was a cherished daughter indeed.

Both Mr. and Mrs. Hendricks were glad to see the back of Uncle Barnaby, whose unruly presence was like a tsunami rushing through this canning town that had only known a gentle seaside breeze. His most catastrophic faux-pas was whisking Jemima away on an excursion to Dithers Landing: perhaps you've been there already? It's the second-best attraction in town, so I'd highly recommend a wander over there this afternoon. Anyway, the trip to the Landing was the only thing Jemima had ever done without her parents' permission. It was a crowded summer's day when Barnaby and Jemima went for their walk along the pier. The tide was out as they strolled along past the fish stalls, where the boats moored in the low water. Fishermen pulled out buckets full of their day's catch to sell on the docks before the rest was shipped to the cannery. This was before they gussied it up for the tourists, so it was a quieter place than the salmon-mad bustle you'll see today on a Saturday.

Barnaby laughed his uproarious, rosy laugh and patted his belly with satisfaction when Jemima asked questions about London. As he doddered along, Barnaby told Jemima about the omnibuses in the streets and the carriages in the park and the people as numerous as prawns are in Dithers. Jemima couldn't help but imagine that everyone in London was as boisterous as her uncle, and she promised herself that she would go with him someday to swim in the Serpentine and sleep on the steps in front of the Prince Albert memorial, the way Barnaby said he often did. I went to London myself once. It was my first and only time out of the country, actually, and I wouldn't recommend it. People ride the underground like they're heading either to Heaven or Hell – all elbows and hurry for the next, better thing, or else they look shrivelled and drooped like kelp away from the sea. Give me a damp fishing town over a world-class city any day. You guys have made a very sensible choice for a vacation spot at this time of year: who wouldn't prefer a light shower over a swooning heat?

During their excursion, Barnaby bought Jemima an ice cream sandwich wrapped in wax paper from an enterprising fisherman who kept an icebox full of confections. Then he lifted her up and spun her around until the sea and the horizon teeter-tottered and the ice cream made its way back out of Jemima and onto an unsuspecting passerby. That's when Barnaby himself stumbled and fell into a chuckling heap at her feet. Instead of getting up he lay down flat on his back in the middle of the dock, looked up at the clouds, and invited Jemima to join him. Mrs. Low from the post office had to step carefully over Barnaby's body in order to get her basket of halibut safely to shore. Such public shenanigans were unheard of on the Landing before Barnaby's arrival, and Mrs. Hendricks in particular was adamant that something must be done before he ruined the family's good name.

The Hendricks did, however, approve of Jemima's other new hobby. The dollhouse was quiet and relatively tidy, and kept her inside, right where they could keep an eye on her. She would take out the scissors, Q-tips, and glue from a dedicated section in her mother's sewing box and set up her craft station by the fire in the drawing room after dinner. As she stitched and glued, her parents would snuggle on the loveseat, rubbing noses, which was the closest they ever got to expressing physical affection in front of their daughter. Jemima found it somehow more embarrassing than actual kissing.

I sometimes wonder what would have happened if Barnaby

stayed to whisk Jemima away on more seaside adventures. Would she have given up miniatures after that first dollhouse? Wouldn't you, if you had a jolly uncle to play with? Jemima wrote in her diary that Barnaby promised to take her dogsledding in the Great White North, snorkelling in the Caribbean, and around the world in a hot air balloon. The voyages he promised had not even occurred to her before, growing up as she did in a pre-television, pre-Internet era here in Dithers, where she attended the one-room schoolhouse across from the cannery. But Barnaby did vanish, as was his way, and so instead of riding camels in Constantinople, or floating across the Atlantic ocean with a steamer trunk, she was left with just the frame of a wooden house and the bare outlines of its inhabitants. Sometimes I can't help but think she spent her life building and rebuilding that summer out of materials she could shape with her own hands.

So, why don't we move along to the next room? Directly beneath the attic is the nursery. As you can see, there are two babies here. The twins. I call them Jessica and Mary-Beth. An interesting fact about miniature babies is that they don't have bodies. They consist only of porcelain heads, swaddled in handmade cloths. The swaddling garments are constructed by splitting a single length of yarn into several individual threads and knitting them together in the usual purl-knit stocking stitch. You can tell that the babies are fraternal rather than identical twins because Mary-Beth has blue eyes and Jessica's are green. Well, you do have to look *very* closely, yes, but they are definitely different. The nurse sits in a corner, reading a book of ABCs, presumably aloud, for the edification of the infants. Imagine how well behaved the babies must be for the nurse to be able to relax like that! The pink paisley wallpaper in this room was chosen by Megan Cunningham, Jemima's dearest childhood friend, who frequently donated supplies to Jemima's work throughout her life. Mrs. Cunningham remains a trustee on the board of this museum to this day and is often consulted on historical matters. Like many witnesses, she has her own biases. The museum needs to keep her happy, of course, but she's not the best person to ask about Jemima's adult life: in fact, they were estranged once Mrs. Cunningham married the local doctor and had children. From Megan's perspective, it was a gradual growing apart, but I have my suspicions. She is well known to be a dreadful correspondent.

When Jemima was sixteen years old, her mother died unexpectedly. Rosalie Hendricks was discovered near the sea by a beachcomber, with a hermit crab clutched in her left hand. Though her father never explained the cause of death to Jemima, I read in the historical newspaper archive that it was a sudden cardiac event. She was still wearing her blue gingham apron when they found her, and she left freshly baked oatmeal cookies on a cooling rack in the kitchen. Mrs. Hendricks's meticulous diaries stop abruptly at this point, obviously. Yet, the day after her death, Jemima wrote a single line in her distinctive pinched cursive: "The world is tired today." You must make of that what you will. But I'm sure you can imagine how moved I was in the archive when I turned the page and found Jemima's own handwriting. It felt like a sudden cool rain after a dusty, parched summer. There was no sign of Jemima writing in the diaries before this moment, but after her mother's death she began to write every day, and not just accounts but her own reflections. At first she wrote brief phrases, but then she began to record her life more fully as the years went on. In my view the early aphorisms are the best, because with fragments you can fill in the meaning yourself, can't you?

The other day I was on the local bus and everyone was yawning, even the driver. I read somewhere that yawns are contagious. Have you guys heard that? Must have been in the "Health" section of the paper. Anyway, I couldn't help but think of poor Jemima and her tired world. I can't get that line out of my head sometimes. Perhaps she meant something more than a bus full of sleepy commuters, but I'm not an authority on such matters.

After the tragedy, by all accounts, Mr. Hendricks carried on carrying on, in the way that men did in those days. He kept the hermit crab shell on the mantelpiece.

Directly beneath the attic, you'll see an artist's studio. Inside is a tiny nude, posing for a miniscule portrait. She sits in a semi-recumbent posture on a burgundy upholstered chaise-lounge and holds out her palm as if she's offering invisible desserts on a non-existent platter. The artist is dressed in grey, paint-splattered clothes, and has what I'm sure you'll agree can only be described as whimsical hair. He holds his brush aloft, just above the painting. To the naked eye, what's on the canvas just looks like random strokes of paint, but if you use the specialized magnifying goggles to the right of the display case, you'll see that it is actually an abstract interpretation of the nude, who appears, half drawn, in bold shapes. I don't know if I'd use the word "monstrous" myself, ma'am, but of course everyone sees modern art differently, don't they? Jemima achieved the detail by painting the image using a brush with a single bristle. Maybe it's a good thing that the sitter can't see the painting. It isn't what you would call flattering. No, her gaze is fixed on the back of the easel, and her wrist just floats there, like a starling that is about to strike a window. It's a departure, as you'll see, from the realism of the rest of the house. You're quite right, sir, it does feel a bit out of place, whatever she's trying to communicate with it. Thank you for saying so. I've often thought the same thing.

In the years following her mother's death, Jemima set about the task of finding Uncle Barnaby. Perhaps it was a way of dealing with her grief, or perhaps it was simply a quest to find the man who had unwittingly discovered Jemima's great talent. Megan Cunningham seems to think that Jemima remained the same after her mother's death, carrying on without mentioning the loss. However, the diaries show otherwise, and if Mrs. Cunningham had bothered to read between the lines at all, well, she'd have a better understanding of how Jemima's grief shaped her work. I'm not one to speculate on these matters, but shortly after her mother's death, Jemima's work took a domestic turn, focusing once again on the detailed interiors of houses, just like the one you see before you. Personally, I think that means something, but Mrs. Cunningham tells everyone I'm over-reaching. As if such a thing is possible when it comes to the intimacy of sorrow! All I know is that I still speak to my mother every day, and I'm an adult. (Though sometimes I think she probably wishes I would leave her alone!) I certainly found that at sixteen I could hardly cope with the idea of death, let alone an actual tragedy.

But I'm getting off topic.

Since Barnaby Supple was a fake name, Jemima had no luck in her quest to find her uncle. Her father was no help, because even if he had known of his brother's whereabouts, he didn't think his daughter should be associating with such a scoundrel. Periodically, she wrote letters of inquiry to Supple residences across North America and in England. Over the years, she received several kind replies offering visits and whiskey and information about other Supple families who would eventually prove not to be related to her at all. One such correspondence, with a gentleman named Adam Supple, a welder from Boston, Massachusetts, lasted three years, and was, perhaps, the greatest love affair of Jemima's life. They wrote to one another weekly for the duration of their acquaintance and met in person only once, for a romantic weekend in Niagara Falls. They went to the world's largest aviary, kissed sweetly among the parakeets, and felt small against the rushing green of the falls. In a fit of passion, Jemima wrote in one of her later letters to Adam that she wished they had jumped off the edge of the falls hand in hand and let themselves spin to the very bottom of the world together. A bit of lovesick melodrama, if you ask me. I'm sure Jemima didn't mean it. Besides, Mr. Supple was a married man with three children, so their affair was not one of consistent physical closeness, but was confined instead to a flutter of envelopes and loops of cursive: OxOxO.

Ma'am, if you'd like to know more you can read the letters from Mr. Supple yourself after the tour. We have a few on display upstairs, but the full archive is available so you can come back and make an appointment. I'd say they're skippable, though. The usual overdramatic declarations of affection. Well, yes, certainly you're right that some people might have chosen to leave Dithers in pursuit of passion, but thankfully Jemima wasn't one of them. Which is probably for the best as it seems that Adam Supple never intended to leave his family, despite what he expressed in his correspondence to his "dear sweet Jemma." Jemima was a diversion in his life, while he was central to hers. I think even if she had left, she would have only faced rejection and disappointment, because isn't that always the way with romantic love? I suppose that's a cynical thing to say, yes. And no, it's true, you and your husband do seem very happy, ma'am. I didn't mean to suggest otherwise. But, the fact is that Jemima chose to stay right here. Certainly, her mother's death had left her the responsibility of caring for her father. But there was another reason she decided not to become a world traveller. Moving's a nightmare at the best of times, but can you imagine with all this? And you guys still haven't been upstairs yet to see the Great Wall of China or the submerged City of Atlantis in the home aquarium. It's true that it was after this affair that her miniatures became ever smaller, but I don't think it was her tiny empire that bound her to this place. She must have loved the oceanic odour and the soft, continual fog. Dithers was, simply, her home.

Sure, I've thought about moving, too. I've considered seeking out work at one of the bigger institutions, the Royal BC Museum, say, because who hasn't at least entertained the possibility of abandoning Dithers? Even my mother has gone to live in Vancouver now, and I'm the only one still here from my high-school class. But I'm a loyal Ditherer. Don't get me wrong: I've had my own chances to take off for something bigger and better. I went to university in Victoria and got scouted by Tiny Town, but I didn't even consider the possibility. I knew I had to come back. And anyway, Tiny Town. They think they're so great. Between you and me, they'll take any random figurine a person donates as long as it's little. No curation standards whatsoever, and who wants to work in a place like that?

On the ground floor, we have an open-plan kitchen and dining area. This was somewhat anachronistic for a Victorian house of the kind that Jemima was trying to recreate here, but she felt strongly about eat-in kitchens as a more sociable layout. It's touches like these that make her miniatures unique. She thought about daily convenience. Anne, the cook, is preparing a roasted pork belly, which, if you'll press the green switch again, you can see – complete with crackling – when the oven light turns on. The copper pots and pans are truly made from copper, since Jemima was learning metalwork during the early 1960s, which was a turning point in the sophistication of her creations. The cook has her back to us and is busy peeling potatoes. Note the ribbons of potato skin strewn in the sink. If you make use of the goggles, you can take a look at her manicured hands – completely inappropriate for a cook, and anachronistic, too. Those bright red fingernails are, I like to think, a feminist statement.

I should mention that Jemima never worked, nor was she ever married, so the transition between her childhood and her adult years is not as clear as it might be in some biographies. Sometimes she was called upon to make dolls on commission for local girls, but it was a modest business and she kept no storefront.

Oh, yes. Please do ask a question! Interrupt me any time, by the way.

No. Goodness, no. She was not a diagnosed obsessive compulsive. But thank you for asking. You raise an excellent point, ma'am, and I want to clarify that what you're viewing is not the product of a mental illness. In public, Jemima was a genial and lively companion, perfectly well versed in the art of conversation. Just ask Mrs. Cunningham. Actually, don't. She doesn't like being asked too many questions. I found that out the hard way. Anyway, when Megan was still taking my calls, she told me that Jemima's research for her various miniatures gave her an admirable expertise in a range of subjects: she knew a great deal about animals, food, European fairy tales, railways, home furnishings from various historical periods, plumbing, electricity, and airplanes. She seemed to think that

Jemima could prattle on a bit sometimes, but I can't tell you how much I would welcome the chance just to listen to her talk! No one thought her strange, and the church community in particular valued her wit, her generosity, and her famous butter tarts. What you see around you is a collection of the harmless sort that you might find among coin enthusiasts or fanatics of Jubilee spoons, only it was made by the hands of an artist.

Mr. Hendricks never participated in the creation of the miniatures, no, but that's a very good question. He worked in the cannery until he retired and often took, according to the diaries, "a long walk amidst the cottonwood trees of an evening." He liked to relax in front of the fire. He never kept any record of his own life, and was not a frequent correspondent, so it is difficult to get a sense of his voice from the historical archive. Our guests do often ask about him, so I wish there was more I could say. At first, he supported Jemima's hobby by buying her spools of ribbon and wire cutters or, in the case of her fourteenth birthday, a mahogany table, which you see here in the dining room. By the time she reached the age of twenty, though, her father had lost interest in the venture, and tried to encourage his daughter to take up baking, sewing, and other full-sized domestic activities that would translate her skills into appropriate wifely virtues. By this time, Jemima was no longer focused on starting her own family, but on continuing the one she had. Mr. Hendricks and his daughter were thrown together, of course, by circumstance. Sometimes, and this does seem a bit embarrassing when I say it out loud, I even pretend that Mr. Hendricks was my father, and that instead of living on my own in my basement apartment on Chatham Street, I live here, with a salty, curmudgeonly, aging dad.

I'm thinking about what more I can offer you about Mr. Hendricks. Thirty years went by and there's almost nothing to say. He was so reticent that he didn't even speak at his wife's funeral. It's safe to say that it was a surfeit rather than a deficit of love that produced his silence. Once, seventeen years after his wife's death, as the early December snow dusted the frozen ground and he and Jemima strolled past the Christmas displays in the shop windows, Mr. Hendricks expressed his regret that they would not be buying their once-habitual gift of a new tree ornament for Mrs. Hendricks. He nodded at a shimmering silver bauble that caught the crisp white sunlight, and said, "I'd have chosen this one." According to Mrs. Cunningham, this was the only conversation Jemima ever had with her father about her mother after her death. Jemima looked after him in this house until he died, at the age of ninety-three, in his sleep.

Now, I must warn you all to prepare yourselves for what is to come. Unfortunately, we have reached the inevitable tragic fall at the end of any life story. Have you noticed that all lives are tragic in Aristotle's sense? No, well, I'm not an expert in the Classics. It's just something I've been thinking about. Anyway, let's get this bit over with so that you can fully enjoy the rodeo later, free from intimations of mortality, shall we?

Jemima died suddenly of a pulmonary embolism just three days after the death of her father. All of her papers were meticulously in order, labelled, and filed in the study alongside her microscope and other implements. She donated her home and the miniatures to the city, and we opened the museum shortly afterwards. Some conservation work was done, but mostly the house was left as she kept it, so you'll see when you get upstairs that the 1001 Nights display is actually in Mr. Hendricks's old bedroom. That room smells, even still, of the sea.

I hope you won't think it indelicate if we take a moment to experience the bathroom together. Oh dear. That came out wrong. I can never quite think of how to say that part without it sounding strange, but you'll forgive me, won't you? It's a marvel of petite engineering. The toilet actually flushes! All the plumbing, like the electricity, is functional. Again, this is a chain-pulling operation if you do it by hand, but we've also automated it for your enjoyment. So, please, ma'am, why don't you go ahead and press the blue button to your right?

Please don't leave! I didn't mean to offend you or your wife. It was just all intended to be light humour, but you're quite right that it was off base after the saddest part of the story. I'm sorry. Please come back. The last room is worth it, I promise.

No, sir, it's very kind of you to say that, but it doesn't look like they're coming back. She's already put on her raincoat. This has only happened once before but I think that time it was an English language issue. How humiliating. I wonder what the problem was? The bathroom is usually a hit! Normally the tour is a take-it-or-leave-it situation; it seems rude to leave in the middle unless there's an emergency. Well, I'll just carry on. No use being put off by the overly sensitive now, is there? Besides, I'm sure we can have more fun now that it's just the two of us.

Now we come to the last room of this magnificent dollhouse, which as you'll see is a traditional parlour with a fireplace. I've saved it for last and I hope you'll see why. It's where the action is happening. It may not map exactly onto the tour as I've given it so far, but you have to allow a little wiggle room with history, don't you? The fire can be lit, but not now, not on the tour. Even I've never seen that done. Far too much of a hazard! Can you imagine? Local heritage home set alight by a pinkie-sized stove! Nevertheless, I won't say I haven't been tempted. Anyway, the chimney would need cleaning.

Oh, look at me! Getting carried away now that it's just the two of us. Your eyes are striking, by the way, has anyone ever mentioned that? I can't decide if they're so blue they're a little bit purple or if you just seem like such a good person that I am embellishing them in my head even as they're staring at me. It almost pains me to look away, but we've been here almost half an hour already and we're still in the first exhibit room, so I guess we'd better get a move on.

I don't normally tell people this, but for you I'll make an exception. When I first started this job I used to stay behind after the others had gone home. To clean up, supposedly, but I just used to get out the keys and open up the display cases. If you reach inside you can run your fingers along the surfaces and come to know all the tiny textures intimately with your hands. Upstairs, there are three different kinds of faux grass on the landscapes, each with its own particular prickliness: soft and barely textured for the undulating prairies; Astroturf of a familiar kind for the football pitch; hard and parched for the Wild West. I can even tell you the eye colour of each figurine, and name the ones with chips and smudges. It seemed so much better than going home, hanging out here and figuring out how each small thing worked. I don't stay late anymore though. At first I was learning so much I didn't notice just how quiet it was. I'd even have settled for Cody's banter when it got really late and all the lights were out on the rest of the block. The figurines don't do enough talking to make you feel like you're getting something back.

Now I'm really rambling. But you don't mind that this is taking a while, do you? You're having a good time? Since it's just you and me left I thought maybe we could even grab some fish and chips later, after the tour? There's a little booth on the boardwalk where they wrap your food up in regular paper disguised as newspaper so you don't get ink in your system. No need to answer now. Take your time: we still have Venice and the Rockies to cover upstairs! You can think as we tour. No pressure. Just enjoy yourself! Anyway, there's just one more thing I want you to see before we move on from this house.

Above the mantel is a painting in the style of the artist upstairs, one of his early works, perhaps, although it appears to be a landscape rather than a portrait. You'll notice that there's a little girl in a green dress with her hair in French braids sitting by the fire with a doll. In the corner is a mustachioed man with a potbelly, holding a glass of brandy aloft, gesturing with his free hand as if he is about to win an argument. On the upholstered love seat are a man and a woman. The woman wears blue gingham, and the man has a long, tangled beard. They sit facing each other, touching diminutive noses.

CIRCUS

☞ SUSAN'S GRANDFATHER WAS A BEAR IN THE travelling circus. Or, rather, he wore a bear. Actually, she is never quite sure how to put this. He wore a bear suit (made from the skin of a real dead bear) and wrestled someone in a wrestler's suit (made out of not very much cloth). In his moments of glory, he reared up on his hind legs (which were his only legs) and roared. One of the first organized animal rights protests in the city of Tunbridge Wells was held in 1910 on behalf of Susan's grandfather, the bear, who happened to be human. This fact was never discovered because the circus was bound to lose business either way: if the ringleader exposed the truth, he would surely lose audiences who took pleasure in watching grappling animals, and, anyway, who wanted to see a man fighting another man in a bear suit? Plenty of people, apparently, as long as they thought at least one of the men was a bear. If, on the other hand, the circus-master kept the fact of Susan's grandfather's humanity concealed, the animal rights activists would continue as they were: pelting innocent tomatoes and cabbages at the Big Top and vandalizing the caravans. The solution was that Susan's grandfather was set free.

To Susan, then, the circus is an Edwardian photograph of cross-dressing midgets with shotguns, whose limbs are being devoured by tigers that are actually people. There are no clowns who make balloon animals in Susan's circus. There is no cotton candy. There are handlebar mustaches, and perhaps there are bearded ladies with real beards. No Ferris wheels, but Siamese twins joined at the head wearing only one jumpsuit. No fishing for little plastic ducks with prizes on their bottoms, but maybe, if you're lucky, a fat and monocled man on an elephant, selling tickets at the entrance to the fairground.

You understand the distinction.

Susan hasn't often fashioned improvisational tightropes out of laundry lines laid out on her carpet so she can practise walking across, as she is doing right now. She hasn't always needed to walk in a straight line. But she's changed jobs recently and she feels compelled to leap up onto a concrete ledge beside a flowerbed on Queen Street West on her new walk to work. There's a sidewalk next to the ledge, sure, but the ledge is just the right height, just near enough to some slightly sad geraniums planted in gravel, to be irresistible. Plus, now that she's started doing it, she can't break the habit. Only she's missed her step a couple of times and it's bad form to arrive at work in a shiny Toronto office building with ladders in her stockings. She keeps a bottle of clear nail polish in her purse in case the domestic tightrope training doesn't actually help improve her balance. Susan has a bit of a problem with perseverance, and already she knows the tightrope phase won't last long enough to make her an expert ledge-walker. She keeps souvenirs from all her momentary and vehement obsessions in shoeboxes (from the shoebox phase) under her bed. A felting phase, a woodcarving phase, a guitar phase (too big for a shoebox, but she keeps the picks), a drawing phase, a Latin phase, a cooking phase (hundreds of recipe cards), a crack-cocaine phase, and a button phase are all from the last six months. She did a neurotic spring-clean last April and killed two birds that way, by storing the rags and cleaning products in the box from her boyfriend's basketball shoes. Susan is already thinking of how to coil up the tightrope so it will fit where her sandals used to.

When her mother talks about her circus days, it is with a kind of dutiful resignation. "Yes," she says, "it was difficult being brought up a bear cub. Harder than you can really imagine, you of a regular human childhood."

Her mother was twelve years old and preparing for a life as a contortionist when Susan's grandfather ceased to be a bear. After they left the circus, however, her father was distraught, and wanted no reminders of his former vocation. So Susan's mother was forced to walk on her feet instead of her hands, and to keep her back in a shape more like a human back than like a snail shell. This was a painful and incomplete adjustment, and from time to time, at boring parties or while Susan's father was at work, she would yawn with her whole body – nonchalantly flipping her back over until her head appeared between her legs. It wasn't about showing off, it was just the way it happened sometimes, and Susan never really blamed her for not being like other mothers. One of Susan's own phases had been contortion. She found that she had none of her mother's natural gift, and sprained her neck, though she refused to get one of those foam things to hold her chin up. Instead she got an empty shoebox, labelled it *Contortion*, stuck it under her bed, and walked around for a few weeks with her head lolling a little to the left.

Leon is Susan's boyfriend. He comes home every day at exactly the right time, even though this is a different time almost every day. Sometimes Susan is already home and sometimes she isn't, but he has a way of opening the door, or of sitting on the sofa in front of the TV, that seems freakishly coincidental. If Susan needs a long bath and some time to herself, he comes home late. If she wants to play cards or make dinner, he's there right at five. Susan's favourite arrival, though, is when they both approach their apartment building at the same time, from different directions, and avoid eye contact as they walk towards the entrance. Then, without speaking, they get in the elevator, cough awkwardly as they ascend, and walk down the hall. When they arrive at their common destination, he presses her up against the door, her head right next to the brass 1216, and they make out as though they are strangers who have just met in an elevator and discovered that they live in the same apartment.

Leon is a marketing executive for a company that makes organic chocolate products. Their apartment is full of tins and wrappers, all dark brown with gold lettering and bars of colour at the edges to indicate flavour. The brown was Leon's idea: "The colour of chocolate," he said at the interview, and so they hired him. Leon mostly ignores Susan's quirks, which is comforting and necessary. When Susan says things that don't make sense, or when she makes sock monkeys for days and days without doing anything else, Leon just rolls his eyes and carries on reading, or shaving, or doing whatever it is he's doing at the time. He does intervene when necessary: he bought a bed skirt to conceal the shoeboxes for when company comes over, and had a gentle word about the crack-cocaine phase before it got too out of hand. Yesterday, he tried to come to her rescue by buying a new pair of loafers and leaving the box suggestively beside the laundry line on the carpet. But Susan is not ready, not yet, to give up on the tightrope.

At her new job, Susan draws cartoons about the apocalypse on a pad of Post-it notes. In her previous job, she also doodled, but she drew the End Times on the backs of invoices for European Hardwood flooring. At the job before that one, she rendered scenes of destruction on the bits of paper that were left for testing pens and highlighters at the University Book Store. Usually the apocalypse involves a lot of ants and, naturally, a spirally explosion with rockets emerging from it. She's not sure how to explain the ants, but they are absolutely vital to the proceedings. They look like the fire ants she saw on her trip to Toronto Island last fall, and they bite. Of course, after the apocalypse they won't have much to munch on, and Susan is sorry about this. She never draws what happens after the apocalypse. She doesn't presume to know. In a graduate English seminar two years ago, Susan met a girl who announced that she "was engaged in examining deconstructionist analyses of post-apocalyptic fiction." This deeply alarmed Susan, who had just declared that she "quite liked Laurence Sterne." The girl's academic interest also had Susan worried that she'd somehow missed the apocalypse. She left the room after an agonizing two-hour discussion about globalization and culture, experiencing a small panic attack as she tried to get out of the building. That day, Leon arrived at their apartment before she did, and greeted her by handing her a wine glass. "It's okay," he said, "you're home now."

She quit her English degree two days later.

Susan often worries about whether she actually loves Leon and whether he actually loves her. There have been signs pointing both ways. Her worry led to a phase last month of picking the petals off daisies one by one, but never saying, "he loves me" or "he loves me not." The last time she did this she was in elementary school and had had no one in mind. This more recent time was much more distressing, and she hated herself for doing it. Still, she sat in front of the TV and picked at the petals, tossing them onto the coffee table one after another, no longer even keeping track, and vowed never to do anything superstitious again. She simultaneously broke and repeated the vow each time she tore off another petal. Leon came home just as she was about to change the channel. He bent over and kissed her hair, then went to the kitchen. He returned with the dustpan and brush, swept the coffee table clean of petals, and emptied them into the trash.

Cartooning the end of the world on Post-it notes is not what they pay Susan to do at this new job, but it may as well be. She sits at a computer all day while hundreds of dots pass across the screen representing numbers. Sometimes she answers the phone, and sometimes she lets it ring. When she first arrived at the job two weeks ago, she tried to make her cubicle more homey by sticking black-and-white postcards to the walls with sticky tack. A starlet dressed in sparkling silver, a team of synchronized swimmers in a star formation, a cowboy straddling a fence. Now the cards fall off slowly, one corner at a time, with a little fluttering sound, onto her desk and her lap and her keyboard. She doesn't put them back up.

Susan doesn't often speak to her co-workers in the cubicles on either side of her, although they sometimes flirt across her, their heads poking out the top of the cubicles like the plastic gophers people beat with soft mallets at fun fairs. Not Susan's kind of fun fairs, of course, but the cotton-candy kind. She often goes to lunch with colleagues but isn't very good with names, so all she can ever manage to think about while trying to eat her sandwich gracefully is whether this man is called "Frank" or "Rick." Whenever anyone says "Susan" she cringes because she feels guilty that he knows her name and she doesn't know his. Mostly people at work think Susan is self-deprecating and shy, but her hunching and shuddering is actually on account of her terrible memory.

As Susan smushes her toes into the carpet on either edge of the makeshift tightrope, she thinks about the manager of her department at work. He'd been unusually talkative earlier today when she met him at the coffee machine, and he'd told her all about his daughter's school play, in which she was going to be a star. "Not *the* star," he said, "an actual star! Her costume is made out of chicken wire! She has five points!" He's an extremely small man, though perfectly formed, and Susan is always tempted to touch his wild, wavy hair, which circles his bald spot like an eagle's nest. She's never actually reached out and done it, though. This is not an attraction thing. "It's just a thing," she'd told Leon last night, who had replied by looking up from his *New York Times* and saying, "Sixteen across: Meddlesome. N _ S _."

"*Nosy*. Don't patronize me," Susan said, without pause.

"I wasn't," he said, circling around the O. "Just drew a blank."

Susan has never been good at crossword puzzles, and has been trying very hard to get better. This is another thing she does at work. There is no shoebox for the puzzles because it's an ongoing quest. Her ex-boyfriend was the best crossworder she'd ever known, and could even do cryptic ones with clues about the Anglo-Saxon word for "helmet" or a type of Gregorian chant or the anatomical term for the space between the upper lip and the nose. She never showed an interest until she was about twenty-five, when her roommates started reading clues out loud at the breakfast table, and she'd felt anti-social for not joining in. Leon had never done a crossword before he met Susan, and now he usually finishes them before she has a chance to see the paper.

Halfway through Susan's thirty-seventh trip across the living room, the phone rings. For a moment, she's uncertain about whether she's allowed to leave the tightrope to answer it. After three rings she jumps and runs to the coffee table, snatching up the phone just as the answering machine beeps in.

"Are we being recorded?" her mother asks.

"I'm afraid so," Susan replies.

For precisely two minutes, neither of them speaks. Susan sighs. Her mother coughs. The answering machine beeps again, and they both say "Hello" at the same time.

"So," says Susan's mother.

"So," says Susan.

"Well. The thing is," she pauses, "you know I miss it."

"I know. What is it this time? Has Dr. Harman seen you?"

"Well, Susan, it's my hip. I've dislocated my hip. Dr. Harman seems to think I can't really manage this sort of thing on my own. So I was wondering. Where's Leon? Is Leon home?"

"He's at work."

"So late? Is he always this late?"

"No. What do you need?"

"I need you to come, just for a week or so. I mean, I imagine a week would just about do it."

"Of course."

They hang up. Susan goes to the bedroom and begins to pack her suitcase. What's in there already is:

One spoon.

One marble hippo, palm-sized.

Thirty-seven cents.

One unused tissue.

A list.

She packs the rest of her belongings and pauses for a minute, her fluorescent pink lacy underwear that she bought as a joke (but secretly quite likes) dangling from her finger. It occurs to her that maybe this has been the apartment phase, the job phase, the Leon phase. She packs as much as she can fit in the roll-along suitcase, and heads to her mother's.

Before she goes, she leaves a Post-it note on the counter.

Contortion accident. Love.

TWO-MAN LUGE

A LOVE STORY

It wasn't the sport I would have chosen. That's the thing about being an Olympian, or any kind of serious athlete, musician, or artist. You don't decide. Maybe your parents do, or your teachers or your coaches or your friends. One well-timed suggestion and the course of your life is set. But it's never really you who makes the call. Many people, I'm sure, can't fully explain why they do what they do for a living. Or they might have a great deal to say, but none of it gets to the heart of the matter. Maybe someone says she became a doctor to help people. But there are lots of useful jobs. Postal workers are immensely helpful, for example. That's why I find it bewildering when people ask: "Why did you become a lugist?" I just don't know how to answer that question. I embarrass myself every time. All those repetitive hours of training, those doleful looks from friends who wanted to hang out during sliding times, and I simply have no answer. I didn't even like toboggans or crazy carpets as a kid, which is a reply I've heard my teammate give. No, luge is not something that occurs to a child when he's at swimming lessons or riding his bike in endless circles in the driveway so his grandmother can keep one eye on him and one eye on *Coronation Street*. Hockey is the stuff of childhood fantasies. Kids dream of snowboarding, skiing, and speed skating, even. But two-man luge?

*

Don't get me wrong: we've always been an athletic family. My dad was a champion hammer-thrower in his day, and my mum is still freakishly good at cartwheels and handsprings from her time as a high-school cheerleader. We went to all the sporting events we could and cheered just as hard for the six-year-olds competing in the potato sack race at the fall fair as we did for the sweepers at the provincial curling championships. So it was just another family outing when my parents, grandparents, and fourteen-year-old me piled into our van and drove to an elementary school in the next town to see my ten-year-old cousin, Jessie, perform in a fundraiser for her Jump Rope Demonstration Team. We cheered her on as we watched her master the double-under, skip backwards with her eyes closed, and kneel atop a human pyramid while turning two ropes in opposite directions. There were little girls bouncing all around, chattering like wind-up toys. They were barely listening to their coach, an older lady who was head-to-toe Eighties in her neon pink, blue, and white tracksuit, with her hair gathered into a voluminous side ponytail. She seemed to be chewing an entire pack of gum with her back molars, which didn't stop her from hollering tips from the sidelines: "Smile, Becky! It wouldn't kill you to grin a little!" The gym was enormous, and the basketball hoops, volleyball nets, and gymnastics equipment were all folded against the walls as if to give centre stage to the event of the moment, the other sports tucking themselves away, quiet as moths. "Baby Love" by the Supremes seemed to be playing on a loop. The girls were performing in small groups all around the gym while their families followed the skippers from station to station. It was like a workout circuit for supportive parenthood.

My cousin's show-off move was "The Wounded Duck," and I whistled as she started jumping with her toes together and then clicked her heels back and forth as the rope swung over her head. It was a wonky, sped-up version of the Charleston, and it was somehow graceless and miraculous at the same time. Jump rope was like that: all about the bravura gesture, the one trick that no one else on the team could perform. One tiny red-headed girl did a somersault into the double-dutch set-up and skipped while sitting on the floor, bouncing her bum over the rope while two other skippers turned the long ropes for her. No matter where you were in the room she was the one you couldn't help watching, the one who held your attention even in a crowd of twenty-odd teammates popping up and down around her. At the end of her routine, she pulled herself up into a perfect bridge position (still skipping), then pushed into a one-handed handstand (still skipping). The crowd stamped their feet and shouted their love, and I found myself spontaneously hollering enthusiasm for her along with everyone else. She couldn't have been older than eleven, but already she must have known that she would always be the best at these tricks. I guess it must have been the same for my dad when his hammer hit the dust way ahead of everyone else's, or for my mum when she stretched out her arms to make her body into a perfect letter *K*. What did it feel like to be so skilled? Would I ever be that good at anything?

While the red-haired girl took a break after her routine to greet her adoring fans, I lined up to make a donation at the pledge table, which was manned by volunteers from the grade five boys' basketball team. They were drawing tattoos on each other's biceps in ballpoint pen and taking turns throwing their empty juice boxes into a distant garbage can as if they were shooting three-pointers. A boy my own age joined me in line and we signed $1 pledges for heart health and received red skipping ropes for our contributions.

"What are you going to do with yours?" he asked, flicking me playfully on the shoulder with the coiled jump rope he'd just been given.

I told him I'd read that boxers use them to stay agile on their feet. I was trying to sound tough, even though my arm was still stinging from where he'd hit me. "And Floyd Mayweather is the best skipper of all time," he said. "True story." He grinned at me as he unfurled his rope and started to skip, first on one foot and then the other, boxer-style. Although he was still a little lanky, he had the swagger of a champion fighter, and his feet danced quick and light as the rope fluttered faster and faster around him like a blur of tiny wings. The way he skipped, his triceps flexing as he pulled the rope over his head nonchalantly, had all the grace and ease and finesse that the little girls lacked. He was literally jumping for joy, which made me want to join in. The more I watched him, the more I felt as though my own feet were hovering just slightly above the ground. Eventually, he twirled the rope to a stop, slung it over his shoulder, and as he gave me a gentle punch on the arm, he said he was glad he'd come to the demonstration.

He said it as if we'd had a choice, but if you knew any eight-year-old girl in the whole Peace River region, even simply by name, who could skip double dutch or cross her arms over or do the grapevine, you were there. Them's the rules. It wouldn't occur to me until much later that I could have said that to him. Made the conversation last a little longer. Still, if I hadn't tagged along with my family for a day of Razzle Dazzles and Turning Rodeos, I wouldn't have met him that first time.

Of course, I'm not the first to question my vocation. There are newspaper editorials all the time attacking the Winter Olympics and questioning what they mean as an institution. Sports like two-man luge, or "doubles luge," as it's sometimes called, get the wrong end of the stick in pieces like this. "Luge: A Death Trap for Dummies?" is my latest favourite headline. "Luge is the fastest and most dangerous of the Olympic sliding sports," the journalist writes, "with athletes travelling at speeds close to 160 km per hour and experiencing centrifugal forces of up to 3Gs – equivalent to those faced by NASCAR drivers – on tight corners. Common injuries include broken bones and concussions. Accidents resulting from poor track maintenance can be fatal. In light of the sport's dangers, we have to ask ourselves: Why are we spending millions of taxpayer dollars so that athletes can slide down icy man-made tracks at ridiculously fast speeds?"

My mum often asks the same kinds of questions. She wouldn't let me play rugby when I was in grade ten because she objected to any sport where you have to tape your ears to your head so they don't get ripped right off. But in luge we keep our chins tucked in to minimize resistance, which doesn't seem so different. There are helmets to protect our noggins, so that's something. I've never been hurt badly, but bruises are part of any athlete's job. For us they blossom in the smalls of our backs, right where the body meets the sled. Of course, there are occupational hazards in any job. I've been lucky; my injuries have been relatively minor, but you never know what's going to happen when you push yourself to be that split second faster. That's the goal, to subtract more and more time from every run so you're speedier than you think you can be. Sure, there's always the chance that you might push it too far, might fly off the track, but you have to take risks if you want a shot at that one great run.

The next time I met the jump-a-thon boy was at a regional track meet three years later. We were both seventeen, nearly through high school by then, and running the 1500m. I loved running long distances on my own. It was a way to test the borders of myself, to see where the ground beneath my feet ended and I began. Eventually, I found it hard to think without the thud of my running shoes striking the track. I liked running until my legs were numb and my body felt as though it were a sort of watermill, moving of its own accord. I liked varying my speed and distances and testing out my legs to see what they were good for. I liked going until I was past my limits and my whole body gave up and I had to throw up in the bushes and stagger home. I even liked circuit training at six in the morning, doing crunches with a twenty-pound weight in each hand, holding the plank position until I buckled, and, yes, skipping rope. I disliked homework, house parties, and snow shovels, which were the other things I spent a lot of time with. I was bad at saying no.

I had no idea how I would do at regionals because I ran by myself every day after school, with just Coach Bradley, his stopwatch, and an enormous bag of Jujubes waiting for me at the finish (though Coach would eat most of the candy, leaving just the black ones for me). The meet took place on a blue asphalt track with the lanes newly painted in white. All the teams were warming up in the soccer pitch in the middle, some wearing matching warm-up suits with their last names embroidered on the sleeves. I wasn't even wearing a school jersey for the race, just a Canucks T-shirt and some old soccer shorts. "I Get Knocked Down (But I Get Up Again)" was playing on a wheezy megaphone, and families were setting up picnic blankets and portable cushions on the bleachers. I could see my mum and dad, sitting beside a Tupperware bin of orange slices that was large enough to fuel a whole team.

I heard him before I saw him, could almost hear the grin in his voice: "True story." He was telling his teammates about a flavour of ice cream that combined bacon and cinnamon, and the eight of them were swinging their legs in circles or bouncing up and down, doing what I would later discover was a plyometric warm-up. My warm-up consisted of a series of static stretches I'd memorized from a handout Coach had photocopied out of an old military fitness book. I sat on the cold ground with my feet sole to sole and my knees pointing outward like French quotation marks, then leaned forward until my nose touched my sneakers. I bobbed up and down a little to intensify the stretch. I know now that my butterfly stretch was disturbingly outdated, exercise science–wise, but I did what I was told. I was wondering if the jump-a-thon boy would remember me when Coach came up behind me and pressed his palm in the small of my back, pushing me deeper into the stretch. "You've got this, buddy. Don't worry about the Eastcreek High jumping beans over there. You've got it." I'm lucky I never tore a hip flexor.

When it was time for the 1500m, the motivational music cut off abruptly and the megaphone crackled our names and schools. The eight of us approached our starting lanes and stood waiting for the horn to sound. The start was my favourite part because the race was all still ahead of you. As soon as you take that first step, the whole sky is in your lungs and you're the one making the world turn under your feet.

He was four lanes away in slot number two. I could just barely see him lean forward, his fingertips on the ground, as we took our marks, poised like jungle beasts ready to pounce. When the horn sounded, I was off. The scraggly groups of parents and coaches and spectators dropped away. The air felt clean and full in my lungs and my breathing was even. All the other runners eventually fell back and grew small in the distance, leaving just the two of us out in front. We were alone, and going so fast there was no visible landscape at all beyond the asphalt surface of the track. In the last few metres he was so close I could hear his heavy breath and actually feel him right behind me. As we crossed the finish line together, they announced our results, first place for me, second for Paresh Banarjee. During the ribbon ceremony, we shook hands and he grabbed my elbow for extra emphasis, like he was happy I'd won instead of him. But I still couldn't tell if he remembered me. I wanted to say something. But what? "Hey, remember me? We met three years ago when we watched those jump-ropers doing the Caboose Shuffle?" Before I could think of something less embarrassing to say, he walked away, and I could only watch dejectedly as he headed back to the bosom of his team. I'd turned to make my way slowly towards my mum, Coach, and the Jujubes when I heard an exuberant, clear voice start to sing "Baby Love." When I looked back, Paresh's whole team had gathered in a huddle around him and joined in as he kept singing, thinking the song was for his second-place ribbon. I nodded back at him, and hummed the saxophone line in response. Then, once again, we went our separate ways.

The only way I can really explain how I got into competitive luge is by talking about inertia. Once you start down the track, there's nothing you can do to stop, even if you want to. There's no pausing the sled and hopping out for a breather or a cigarette or a pee break or a little reflection on life. But if you can stay calm and completely in sync with another person for just under forty-five seconds, before you know it the race is done, and your left ankle is wobbling from an old injury you pretend doesn't bother you, and then you're up, sled in hand, and sliding off the ice track. After some heats, you leave the track slowly with your head hung low, like Charlie Brown, staring mournfully at your aerodynamic booties. At other times, you hoist your sled up above your head like it's the Stanley Cup. But that's competitive sports for you.

The spring before I graduated high school, Coach showed up at our house, interrupting the dinner hour to place a crumpled brochure for a winter sports recruitment camp in my mother's hand. "This is serious, Mrs. O'Farrell. Could be the chance of a lifetime. He's no runner in the competitive world, not beyond high school the way he's growing up. But winter sports are a real possibility. We've got to put those beefy shoulders to good use." To give him his due, Coach was very persuasive in convincing my parents that sports would "open doors" for the future. ("There are scholarships!" he said, chowing down on the cookies my mum had offered him.)

"Is this something you want to do?" my mum asked, and I'd said yes, though I had no idea, really, what I wanted.

During my first week at the camp, I made my first slide on the ice track. I held on tight as an experienced lugist settled me into the sled and then climbed in himself. He grabbed the start handles on each side of the track and pulled the two of us forward and back and forward and back and forward and back. Then he gave a final pull and we were launched out into the half-pipe tunnel, the coach's helmet resting just beneath my chin. I couldn't help but close my eyes. All our velocity seemed to settle in the back of my neck and I held on to that feeling, anchored it there, and for seventy-five seconds I was less a person and more a straight bolt of light, disappearing into the track. Even on the first try, I felt like the Flash. The screen at the finish blinked 65 km/h. Not bad for a first run, though with practice I'd eventually reach speeds of at least 145 km/h. The coaches assigned me to the two-man team for competition, too. If you'd asked me before the sports camp, I would've said I wanted to do singles luge, to be alone out there on the ice like I was on the running trails. But once I realized how it felt to add another person's weight to the ride, there was no going back. The only thing better than the kiss of the speed is having someone else whiz around the track with you.

It wasn't until I was leaving the training centre for the night that I discovered that Paresh also had been enrolled in the winter sports camp extravaganza. I saw him standing by the entrance of the Ice House, chatting with an ice dancer who trained in the rink next door. His cerulean speed suit gleamed against the corrugated iron siding of the building and his neck was arched slightly downward, as if he had wandered out of Picasso's blue period. I didn't want to interrupt, so I just gave him a little nod as I passed, but I hoped more than anything that he would be my partner, and that we could spend our lives careening down icy slopes together. The thought of it made all the hair on my body stand at attention. Imagine the dead feeling, then, of all those hairs flopping right back down in the lawn chairs of my pores when I realized that my partner would, in fact, be a gruff former javelin thrower with veiny arms and a face pocked with acne scars. Ron was twenty-three and had been on the team for five years. His previous teammate had quit luge to study engineering at university, so Ron was in need of a new partner.

Ron had a habit of arriving at practice wearing a yellow Hawaiian shirt printed with small umbrellas and green plaid pajama bottoms over his training clothes. His outlandish wardrobe alone lent him an air of lovable eccentricity, and when he laughed, which was basically every ten seconds, his eyebrows shot up like the ones on a ventriloquist's dummy.

"So, you're gonna be a luger?" Ron asked when we met.

"Isn't is *lugist*?" I said, missing the joke.

"Luger! Loser! Get it? Ha!"

Ron's theory was that you had to own the teasing, otherwise your buddies from home would hassle you all the way to the Olympics. He nudged me and winked in an exaggerated way. "We play it up in public so they can't give us crap. Give 'em what they want to see and forget about it. Cool?" He put his arm around me and kissed me jokingly on the cheek.

I didn't know what to say. I could feel my ears burning. "Cool," I said, after a long silence in which I managed to wriggle my way out of his embrace.

"No, dude. Don't blush. That's, like, the *worst*. You might be a natural at the athletic shit, but I can see we'll be training you on the comebacks."

Don't get me wrong: Ron and I had some good times on the

track, and he was a nice guy and everything, but he didn't have Paresh's sparkle or charm. He didn't, as far as I knew, have a history of attending elementary school jump rope contests and remembering all the words to the songs. But as the top man on the sled, Ron was in charge of the major steering, the kind that meant we wouldn't hurtle around a corner to our deaths. So that was important, obviously. Safety first.

Ron's unwavering friendliness meant that our dorm at the athletes' village quickly became the social centre for all the winter sports teams. We didn't get much free time in our training schedules, but whenever he got the chance, Ron would turn up the music and start a party. On those weekends, Ron left our door unlocked, so people would come in and out at all hours, and, after a while, no one even thought to ask if they could eat things out of our mini-fridge or do physio exercises on our floor or treat my bed as a couch. There were frequently banana peels all over the place because Ron liked to offer everyone snacks. "Gotta fuel up!" he'd boom, hugging his armful of fruit close to his body. "Carbs make dreams happen!"

It was like living on the set of a sitcom, except that instead of producing witty jokes about my boss and being greeted with canned applause, I was the guy who came around to adjust the sound equipment and then grumpily shoo the cast off set. I needed to keep to my sleeping schedule, because if I lost even a fraction of a second of sleep, I might gain that fraction of a second on the track. I thought the way our coaches had trained us to think. Still, I continued to hope our ridiculous thoroughfare of a residence would one day entice Paresh to come see us. He had been picked for the bobsleigh team. The scout who ran the camp put us on the same sort of surface but in different vehicles. I still hadn't actually talked to Paresh – not during the recruitment camp or during the long training period that followed – but I let myself believe he wanted to see me as much as I wanted to see him.

If you wish for something without doing anything to make it happen, you're leaving too much to luck. Paresh didn't stop by any of Ron's parties. He never showed up to drink milk straight from the carton or shadow box against a ski jumper, and I hardly saw him at training. But I came to know his body so well from a distance that I could tell him apart from all the other athletes no matter how far away he was, which is no mean feat in identical suits like ours. I consoled myself with the thought that if I didn't live here, I wouldn't come to these shindigs either. I would be in bed, visualizing Ron and me prerolling into a dished curve on the track. I also spent a lot of time thinking about what Paresh might be up to at any given moment. Since I didn't know much about him beyond his having a reasonably tuneful singing voice and a certain level of athletic prowess, my fantasies of him making up his own dance routines alone in his dorm room probably didn't map so well onto his actual activities. Nor did my hope that he was imagining what I was doing all the time, and, like me, was just too shy to do anything about it. After a couple of months of waiting, I began to focus on the broken hearted part of "Baby Love." That is a rough break, by the way, as far as songs to have stuck in your head for three years running.

As competitive athletes, our days are decided for us. Every day at the training ground is more or less the same. We practise our starts in the morning, taking off over and over again on a little shortened track that ends almost as soon as you and your partner are in the sled. After the starts we do everything we possibly can to make ourselves stronger, which means hours of weights or cross-training. In the afternoons, we do full runs together on the long track. We measure time in 1/1000ths of a second, but each forty-five-second run holds countless hours of work inside it. With every passing year, each run we take holds the weight of more and more time. After a while, you can feel all the hours spent building upper body strength, monitoring our food, and fashioning ourselves into the perfect lugists accumulating, building up, hard as muscle under our skins. Eventually, if you follow all the instructions, even learning to breathe in a rhythm with your partner, you begin to feel like an extension of the sled. Let's face it; humans are not the best at speed. Machines have us beat every time. So I do everything I can to make the mechanics of my own body as efficient, graceful, and invisible as possible. The more your body instinctively knows what to do, the more you feel like you're part of the motion. You become part of the sliding machine, and everything else is a blur. Once you get used to this blurring, you soon discover this is actually a much easier way to live: no looking up, no distractions, no worrying about what's outside your immediate field of view.

Now that I've let go of even the desire to be independent, the speed feels purer and tenser than ever before. It's almost nuclear, as if our bodies, our strength, our will power – everything we've been saving up for our runs – is constantly threatening to split like an atom and peel off in all directions. But once you're in the sled, and you can finally let go, all of it explodes with almost cartoonish power, with the POW! of a comic-strip battle, all colour and brightness and superhuman ability. I really feel that power surging through me when I'm on the track, even if it seems ridiculous when I'm dressed in my street clothes. But you can't have Superman without Clark Kent, can you?

In the lead-up to the Vancouver Olympics, Ron loved to imagine us getting what he called "The Bling." He even made us choreograph a victory dance in case we made it to the podium. It involved me standing in appreciation, trying to slouch and make rapper hands while he pretended to krump by smashing an imaginary watermelon on the ground and yelling "Boom! That's *right*, Canada!" We'd done the pretend victory dance so many times that I occasionally found myself spontaneously slouching and body rolling when I was mixing my post-practice protein shake.

We had a good thing going by the time we got to the Whistler Sliding Centre, Ron and I. We'd reached another level of competitiveness when I learned how to shift my shoulders in perfect unison with Ron's body, and to let myself slide blindly down with him, seeing only the very edges of the track in a blur of peripheral vision. Only the top man can really see, which is why Ron steers. As the bottom man, it was my job to make the small changes, the minute adjustments that could earn the hundredth of a second difference between a decent time and one that would fail to qualify us for the next race. It didn't take long for my shoulders to know instinctively what to do to make the right tempo happen in the straight stretches, to feel the slightest shift in Ron's leg and compensate immediately. So every time we went out to do some sliding, we were superheroes swaddled in the same cape, hurtling our way to oblivion. Usually, I could block everything out but Ron and the sled and the track because I was inside the speed until the run was over. When we finished our second run, though, the applause from the crowds was too much to ignore. After 41.78 pure, clean seconds, our first Olympic competition was over. We'd competed in front of spectators before, of course, but the crowds on the luge circuit are nothing compared to those at the Olympics. The cheering was so booming that the mountains around us seemed to be joining in. We placed eighth in the race, right behind the other Canadian doubles team, who came in seventh. It was basically the result we'd expected. Ron decided that in spite of our lack of Bling we should krump anyway, so we did, right by the finish line, in front of everyone, and the bellow of the crowd expanded and enclosed us. Ron was just what the cameras wanted. He came across as what my grandmother would affectionately call a "character." He said "WOOoooo! That's *right,* Canada!" into the cameras just as he'd planned and held up the athlete's identity card that he wore around his neck like it was a gold medal.

My parents were in the audience for our event. Instead of an orange grove, this time mum had packed a massive red foam finger with a maple leaf printed on the palm, which looked enormous on her tiny hand as she waved it at me after the race. Coach was there, too, wearing a full suit of Olympic clothing in place of his usual NBA track gear. He looked like he was ready to keel over with pleasure as he handed me a bag of unopened Jujubes. I got all the colours this time. He kept hugging my dad, who made no move to return the affection, and wore nothing festive but the crow's feet by his eyes. They were so proud it didn't even matter that we were standing there beside them, rather than up on the podium where Team Austria now stood. As if I was still lying in the sled, I closed my eyes and felt the swell.

Our race was early in the Olympic schedule, which meant that we were allowed to do what we liked for the rest of the games. After the over-scheduled days of training, it was a strange sort of freedom, and I felt adrift within hours of finishing the race. What was I supposed to do now? What I needed were instructions for how to have fun. Around me there were concerts and fireworks and strange unidentifiable mascot creatures holding up their maple leaves to flutter in the wind. It was as if the super-bright technicolour of sliding was starting to bleed into the black and white of everyday life. The first night after our event, I went drinking with Ron and even stayed out later than the rest of the team. For once, I wasn't the grumpy sound guy. I was another character altogether, bobbing along to the music with Ron, who wrapped a giant Canadian flag around us and sang along with Beyoncé. I flirted with a bartender, who grilled me about why I was into luge. "I'm not," I found myself saying, "I'm into dancing!" and shimmied my shoulders, dipping my head back to inhale an acrid hit of smoke machine air. We stayed so late and drank so much that I was sick in the snow. The last thing I remember is Ron propping me up against him and steering us back to the athletes' village.

On Day 10 of the games, slightly wilted by a hangover, I went for a run that lasted an entire morning. I wasn't running to keep up with my training, I just wanted to get back into myself, to shake my muscles loose after the event and feel the ground beneath my feet. I jogged in loops around the ski resort, weaving between tourists on the boardwalk, trying to find stretches of space to be on my own. Eventually, I came to a steep hill and started climbing it, working from my hips and quads, and pushing my way upwards against the wind. It was hard, for once, to focus exclusively on the tightening of my legs and the rough ground under my shoes. All I could think was that I was jump-a-thon good at something now. The world had just told me so. But was that enough of a reason for Ron and me to continue sliding for another four years, and maybe another four years after that? The German team, who won bronze this time, had been together for almost sixteen years. Looking at those guys, I could see how all those forty-five-second intervals can add up: to years that glide past before you even notice what is happening. What would it be like to keep track of time some other way? The higher I climbed, the more it became clear that simply carrying on, letting life whiz past me, would not be good enough. If I stayed in the sport, I would have to make that decision for myself. I needed to pause the sled long enough to decide if I really wanted to keep going.

After I finished my run, I procrastinated by Experiencing Whistler. I bought a miniature bottle of maple syrup shaped like a maple leaf and drank it. It was kind of gross and kind of delicious all at the same time. I went into a gift shop to browse and examined some novelty shot glasses on the bottom shelf of one of the many Olympic souvenir displays. The nylon tracksuit rustle of another athlete approaching made me turn around. Paresh was standing a few feet behind me in his Team Canada gear, browsing through a revolving rack of postcards and tapping his foot to some rhythm in his head. I had given up on ever seeing him again, so I just stood there. He was close enough to touch. I held still for a moment longer, counting down from forty-five in my head. Then, I stepped forward and hugged him. As soon as my hands left their rightful place in my pockets, I couldn't believe I'd done it. But then he hugged me back, and once more with feeling. I took another breath, reached for his hand, and, without saying a word, led him out of the store and into the snow.

BROTHERS

TOGETHER THE BROTHERS PERFORMED, IN THEIR slow and quiet way, the same daily duties they had carried out for nearly forty years. They tended the sheep, delivered new lambs, and coaxed ancient ewes through their last breaths. Willie was in charge of the clippers during shearing season, and George whistled complicated commands to the dogs. Sometimes it was hard to tell that the brothers were two separate individuals, since they always walked close together across the land, as though they were loosely conjoined twins, George's free hand clutching one of Willie's suspenders for guidance. Their practised way of moving was born out of necessity, though, since George was blind, and Willie was deaf.

In the way of people who have long dealt with animals as working creatures, George and Willie felt about the sheep just as they did about the prairie sky and the fences they had built around the fields. Neither brother had ever understood how people could have relationships with animals as if the beasts had human personalities. No member of the flock had a name, and George and Willie neither mourned nor celebrated the creatures' life events. George liked to joke about a cattle farmer they'd met at the fall fair, who had practically written two-volume biographies of his cows. "I wouldn't be surprised," he would say, "if the Murphys had a bovine section in the family photo album." But George never looked into their own sheep's faces and Willie never came to know their voices. They cared for the animals only as was their duty. If ever one of their flock escaped, the two men lumbered slowly after it, so attuned to one another's movements that they hardly ever stumbled. At their age, they seldom caught the strays, but it was in their interest to see that none of their practices changed even though their bodies grew frailer as they neared the end of their eighth decade in the world. If anything, over the years George and Willie became more confident shepherds, and would tell anyone who cared to listen just how they managed, year in and year out, to see to it that everything was done properly, each praising the other's handling of the animals and placing the accomplishment squarely on his brother's shoulders.

The two men haven't always minded this flock. In their youth, they worked for the Texas Ranger Division and were paid a dollar a day for their services, which, they often said, was more than they were worth. Presumably they chased down criminals and shot rifles and possibly even pursued Bonnie and Clyde (the timing would have been right), but no one knows much for certain about their doings in law enforcement. They left the States nearly fifty years ago, thinking they'd head to Alaska to prospect for gold. Sure, the Last Great Gold Rush had more or less lost its sparkle by the end of the nineteenth century, but the brothers were convinced that there was still work to be done in the North, cleaning up what the stampede of hapless money-grubbers had left behind. They had driven up to the border, on through the Peace River, and then followed an old fur trader's route to Fairbanks, almost four thousand miles from Texas. Like their Ranger days, their gold-mining period remained in some silent place in the brothers' history. Since George and Willie preferred to stick to the shared piece of personal wisdom that it was better to live in the present than to dwell on the past, no one knew how they built their rumoured fortune or what they really did during their decade in Alaska. Maybe they had worked in a mine, or actually struck gold, or maybe they had robbed a bank. Despite the fact that they didn't like to gloat about their worldly affairs or live in a way that suggested any kind of true wealth, there was a consensus among the locals that there had been great triumphs in the brothers' past.

When George and Willie left Fairbanks, they thought that they were on their way home to Texas as they drove down the Alaska Highway in their black station wagon. Instead, they stopped at Mile Zero. On account of the car, James Callahan the saloon owner had first thought that the brothers were undercover agents on serious international business. Since they were not actually spies, they took up work on Samson Jacobs's farm when he needed help tending his sheep after his own brother died following a mishap with a combine harvester. They'd planned to stay for a week while he found someone else, then two weeks, and after a while they stopped talking about leaving. "We liked the folk of the Peace on the way up, and I guess we liked 'em just the same on the way down," Willie would say with a wink, exaggerating his softened drawl. For forty years they remained on their own, no other family, no land of their own, and, after a time, no Samson either, with only the sheep to attend to and no problems to speak of. They saw themselves as the last holdouts of a dying profession, and Sandra Bird, the Hutterite woman who sometimes spun their wool into yarn, assured them that there had been no one in living memory who could match the skill and grace that the brothers brought to the job.

Karen has the face of someone who has swan-dived into love and never hit the bottom. Her eyes are blue and quite round, and her long dark hair is always in an artfully disordered arrangement on the top of her head. She is slim and wears plain, dark sweaters with skinny jeans, and there is a vulnerability about her that is most apparent in her delicate hands, which flutter and weave like sparrows as she speaks. Neither of Karen's children looks anything like her. They are confident and plucky and olive-skinned like their father, and they cheerfully introduce themselves to strangers. Lately, they have taken to making up silly stories about their own lives and introducing themselves by false names. Sally's favourite thing to say is that she's twenty-three and works in a pet store. Karen is not sure whether to be amused or worried about the fact that, in addition to pretending to be in her twenties, her nine-year-old girl has suddenly become flirtatious: Sally has taken to wooing waiters in family restaurants by writing love letters on her napkins and tucking them under the tip. Six-year-old Jackson's imagination is more whimsical, and his preferred way of introducing himself is as a cowboy who rides a blue horse.

Sally and Jackson are playing together upstairs now, in the new master bedroom, with a cardboard box that has become a police station. Downstairs in the kitchen, Karen cradles her cellphone between her cheek and her shoulder, and draws the curtains despite the daylight, because she is trying to keep a secret about their new house from her kids.

"When a person buys real estate, she doesn't expect to arrive at her new home, exhausted after a long drive, to find out that she has not only bought a house, she has also purchased two elderly shepherds."

"I'm sorry, ma'am. I assumed you knew."

"How, Karl? How would I know?"

"Well, Mrs. Schmidt, they were there when we viewed the property."

"I assumed they would move out with the previous owners. I assumed that they were employed by the previous owners and that my purchasing the property would terminate their employment. That seems to me to be a fair assumption."

"I guess things don't work here like they do in Toronto."

Karen has been suspicious of Karl Kinder from the beginning, when she drove up to the local real estate agency and discovered that the real estate company ads – featuring a photo of Karl with his too-big smile and his slicked-back hair and the slogan "The Only Man for the Job" – were everywhere because he was literally the only person who worked in the town's only realtor's office.

"I wish I could laugh at your joke."

"I'm not trying to be funny, ma'am. They worked for Mr. Samson Jacobs and then for Mr. Jacobs's son and his wife, the landowners before your good self. Those brothers have been there since nobody knows when. It's their home. Anyway, they take care of the grounds free of charge, so you won't have to trouble yourself with the maintenance."

Karen can see the brothers now through the large picture window of her new kitchen. They seem to be shearing the sheep's bottoms while awkwardly cuddling each other. "Listen, Karl. I want this situation dealt with. I don't care how you do it, but you have to get them out."

"Mrs. Schmidt, why don't you just go on down and introduce yourself properly? They'll be happy to see you. They really are nice fellas. Also, if it's not an impolite question, what were you going to do with that enormous flock of sheep yourself?"

Seeing that the conversation is going nowhere, Karen hangs up on Karl and punches the door of the refrigerator. The stainless steel turns out to be unforgiving. As she nurses her throbbing fist, opening and closing her hand to make sure that all of her fingers still work, Karen wonders for the umpteenth time since she pulled up to the house in the moving van this morning how she wound up in this godforsaken place. It's true she had felt pent up in the trendy Liberty Village loft where she and James had been living since they got married, so once they knew they'd be moving to rural Northern British Columbia with James's promotion, she hadn't thought much about the precise geography of their new home. She had simply imagined that she would grow proportionally with her new house, like one of those foam capsules from the Dollar Store that, dropped in water, blooms into a toy dinosaur. As it was, Sally and Jackson shared a bedroom, and she had devised more systems of organization for papers and toys and kitchen stuff over the years than she cared to count, because for all its sleek lines and its post-industrial design aesthetic, their downtown condo wasn't terribly practical for a family of four. What was most upsetting was having sex in silence while the kids slept in the open loft bedroom above. It had become a ridiculous mime show, and James's face contorted with a pleasure she couldn't hear was one of the saddest sights she could imagine.

The dream home she had imagined floated by itself on a generic prairie landscape, like a giant unmoored houseboat with only her family on it. When she travelled west on her own three months ago to find a house, *this* house, she had looked out this window and seen the world as though it were a Rothko painting: broad strokes of blue and yellow-green. A single sheep wandered into the tableau and made an endearing ornamental bleat. When she peered out at the fields and couldn't see their edges, she felt a rush of openness, as though the pastures were as deep as they were wide. The house was finished perfectly: the kitchen cupboards were robin's egg blue with small round knobs, and Sally's room had a secret door at the back of the closet that was sure to delight her. There was a quaintness about the town itself, the way it had just one of everything – one gas station, one grocery store, one pub – that initially seemed pleasingly minimalist. She had failed to notice the wind turbines along the highway on the drive from the centre of town to the property, because she'd been distracted by the buffalo waddling about the farm in their big, slow way, nudging one another and lying down like sleepy, picture-book giants.

She runs her hand across the butcher-block countertop in the middle of the south-facing kitchen, tracing her fingers over what had seemed on that first house-hunting visit like acres of prep space. Somehow, the room is smaller than she remembers.

When they finally arrived at the house, Jackson leapt gleefully from the van and pointed at the sheep plodding about the pasture in the distance.

"Mum, are those *our* sheep?"

"No, sweetie, they're . . . Well, actually, I don't know who they belong to, but they're not ours."

"I'll take care of them! I'll take them for walks!" Jack was pumping his fists with excitement.

"You don't take sheep for walks, Jack," Sally weighed in. "They do their own walking."

"I bet they feel baaaaaad," said Jackson. Just as Sally began to laugh so hard she sounded like a love-sick donkey, Karen saw the shepherds for the first time, ambling across the pasture behind the sheep. "Okay, guys. Inside! Time to explore the new house!" She kept her voice deliberately bright and clear as she squinted into the distance to make sure she wasn't hallucinating the brothers.

To finally arrive on the otherwise unspoiled rural property she had fantasized about for months and was so relieved – overjoyed, even – to have found, only to discover the land (though not the house itself, thank God) already inhabited by crazy old men, to find trespassers in her idyll, to find herself in a real place that could be located on any map, with its own sleazy realtors – well, it all seems like an especially cruel joke. She isn't sure what her husband will do when he hears about the problem, but as she watches one of the brothers adjust his suspenders while the other leans precariously against his shoulder, she picks up the phone, dials their old number, and waits to find out.

Willie was six-foot-two and wore large plastic-rimmed glasses with perpetually foggy lenses that often fell halfway down his nose. His neck was bent like a swan's and his clothes hung in a billowing way off his emaciated body. His hair was a salt-and-pepper cloud hovering above his head and this gave him an appearance of calm that his short temper did not bear out. George, on the other hand, was an exceptionally small man whose stature seemed to vary with his mood. At his tallest and most confident, he stood at about five-foot-six, though most of the time he appeared to be a petite five-foot-three. He wore the same sized work pants as Willie, the difference between their physiques somewhat corrected by the complicated system of suspenders Willie had devised to hold the pants up. The pants were purchased at the local Peavey Mart in the same aisle as the steel-toed boots and flannel shirts that the two men also wore. These garments were made of the kind of canvas that delivered so thoroughly on its promise of durability that the shirts and trousers gave the impression that they would outlast the men who sported them.

Willie was the older of the brothers by three years, and although he had lived a marginally longer life and had been given certain advantages that George never received when they were growing up, it was generally assumed that George was secretly the wiser of the two, having an outgoing way about him that made him seem like the natural leader. This was unexpected not only because George was the younger brother, but also because his blindness had him literally following Willie's every step. There was, however, something about his smallness and his certainty that made George the one who took charge, and after all, he hadn't always been blind, just as his brother hadn't always been deaf.

Willie's hearing had disappeared overnight. There was no logical explanation. He went to bed one night shortly after his fiftieth birthday and woke up the next morning entirely deaf. His only medical intervention into the problem was to have George drip tar into his ears every so often, which is what they did when a sheep had an infection or a wound that needed cauterizing. Needless to say, this didn't do much for the deafness, but it did produce in Willie a feeling of pleasant seclusion inside the newly sealed chamber of his own head. George's affliction was much slower. His vision grew gradually worse over several years until, by the time he was sixty, he could no longer recognize objects or walk in a straight line. It was difficult to say which was harder to bear, slow deterioration or rapid trauma, but the brothers were stoical in this as in all matters, and considered themselves darn lucky, in any case, to have each other.

*

"Sweetheart, there's something the realtor neglected to mention about the house."

"Oh? Oh." James steels himself for news of rotten foundations, blocked plumbing, a flooded basement.

"There are two old men living on the property in that old shack down by the pasture."

"What, you mean homeless guys? Or wait, what did Sally tell us is the politically correct term now? Urban outdoorsmen. Although I guess it's not so urban there. Outdoorsmen? That doesn't sound right."

"Not exactly. Apparently, they're shepherds and they take care of the grounds and the animals. Apparently, they've been living here for a long time. Possibly even their whole lives. They look as if they might be related. Brothers?"

"Okay, now you're making this up."

"Honey."

"So we're just supposed to . . . what? Ignore them? Accept them? Befriend them? What is the right thing to do here?"

"Kick them out!"

"Are they really going to bother you that much?"

"Me? What about us? Our kids? You? We don't know these men at all and they look like they've done their share of living. You know what Sally's like. She'll be down there with muffins from her Easy-Bake Oven and friendship bracelets for them before the week is through. Anything could happen, James."

"Should I catch a plane tomorrow? I can probably finish tidying up here tonight."

"I guess? I really don't know what to tell you. I had some stern words with our friend Karl and he didn't seem to think there was a problem."

"He says they're okay?"

"Sure, but should we really be trusting his moral judgment at this point?"

"What do the kids think?"

"They haven't seen the shepherds yet. They're too busy playing police station. I think they're still a touch weirded out by the move, but I'm doing my best here."

"Fair enough. Okay. I'll let you know when I have a flight."

Speaking to James instinctively makes Karen relax her shoulders from their previously garbled stress-posture. After all, there is bound to be some kind of solution to the problem, and James is good at dealing with crises. For the first time in several years, Karen considers going out to the liquor store to buy a bottle of whiskey so that she can sit in her new kitchen and drink a glass on the rocks.

After a few minutes of savouring the imaginary zing of alcohol and the bliss of ice on her tongue, Karen opens her eyes and notices a worrying quiet about the house. She leaps out of her chair and bounds up the stairs two at a time to check on Sally and Jackson, suddenly feeling in the base of her throat a worry that she knows will not go away until they are all settled and the shepherd situation is resolved. The relief she feels at seeing the two of them asleep, curled up on a double sleeping bag, still wearing their shoes, is so powerful that it makes her sink to the floor. She kneels there for a few minutes, wondering if she should wake them for dinner since they haven't eaten since lunch, but her body is cold in the way that comes only with total exhaustion. Once she starts to yawn she can hardly stop her eyelids from shutting. Karen lies down on the sleeping bag, snuggles between her children, and falls asleep.

One of the advantages that Willie had been afforded as the eldest son of the family was a Classical education. He was privately tutored in dead languages until the age of seventeen, by which time he had mastered Latin and some Ancient Greek, and memorized a number of Horace's Odes, which he could recite in a slow and meticulous Latin.

Dissolue frigus ligna super foco
large reponens atque benignius
deprome quadrimum Sabina,
o Thaliarche, merum diota.

He would intone these lines to the sheep, or to the sky, or to the fences, or to George. He had never recited the poems to anyone who actually understood a single word he said, but his memory was keen and accurate, and the thought of his voice profiting on his hours of hard labour in the study of his father's scholarly friend was reassuring, even if he couldn't hear the sounds himself anymore. Willie filled notebooks with his own Latin compositions, lines and lines of illegible verse on subjects he kept to himself, and over the years he amassed a great many of the little brown books, which he gathered in a leather suitcase he kept underneath the roll-top writing desk that sat between the brothers' beds in the middle of their small house. There were times when he contemplated throwing the notebooks away or leaving them somewhere in town, at the library, perhaps, for someone else to find. They were the only unnecessary possessions that fettered him to the world, excluding, of course, the desk itself with its accompanying cups full of pens and the beautiful if faded writing mat made of stiff linen that covered its surface. A sweetheart of Willie's had sewn this for him back when he used to take women out and bring them home with him. She had seen the desk with its uneven surface and, wanting to smooth it out, immaculately measured the width and depth and made the mat with exquisitely flat seams to fit the desk just so, and Willie was more grateful for this than for any other thing a woman had ever done for him. That he usually found emotional attachments to objects just as incomprehensible as the overly fond relationships that other people had with their pets, and that George frequently mocked him for his peculiar obsession with the things associated with his own learning by calling him "Professor" when he was up to his elbows in sheep placenta, were two of the reasons why Willie sometimes wanted so strongly to get rid of the notebooks. Somehow he could not bring himself to do it.

When Karen finally wakes at eight the next morning, she is still wearing her clothes from the day before. Sally is asleep, and Jackson is sitting cross-legged at the foot of the sleeping bag staring at her. Karen nods at him drowsily and tries to figure out if it is possible to really be awake yet, or if she should set him up with a book and go back to sleep.

"If we're all going to die, why are we born anyway?" Jackson asks.

"Go back to sleep," she says, rolling over and closing her eyes. She has strange and horrible dreams about losing her keys before waking fifteen minutes later to find Jack still sitting there, expecting an answer.

"It's all going to be okay, Jack."

"I know," he says, raising one eyebrow and looking at Karen sidelong. He hadn't been seeking reassurance.

"Well, I think we'd better go have some breakfast. Come to the store with me and get the makings for pancakes?"

"Chocolate chip pancakes with Mickey Mouse ears?"

"Done deal."

As Karen gets ready to go, she considers waking Sally. Jack is already by the door, waiting. She would like to let her daughter sleep, but there's nothing here to eat, so she lifts Sally up gently and carries her out to the car. Karen cannot answer questions about why people are alive without at least the consolation of chocolate chips, which seems, at the moment, like as good a reason as any.

*

When Willie looked up over the sloping field to the grand house at the edge of the road, he was never quite sure how to feel about it. George hadn't laid eyes on the place in many years, of course, and since he was given to a less nervous disposition, its state never worried him in the first place. Willie often wondered, in fact, whether worry itself was what a person gained by learning to read and write, and he noted in himself a kind of wobbliness of sentiment that had no part in George's everyday contemplations. So it was that Willie was the only brother to pay any attention to the changes of ownership that were taking place on the property on which they had, after all, become trespassers. The previous owners, Mr. Jacobs Jr. and his wife, were a childless couple who kept to themselves. They inherited the property from Mr. Jacobs Sr., who had insisted in his will that the brothers be allowed to remain where they were. Although they employed the brothers for years, the Jacobs had left them more or less alone, happy to avoid having to deal with the flock. They had also, Willie suspected, been unwilling to disturb the lives of two old men who had become a crucial part of the town's story.

Over the years, Willie had watched the house from a distance, as it transformed from a kind of stately old grandeur to an emblem of modern convenience. The aging carpets had been torn out and replaced with hardwood, the roof redone, and the whole exterior painted in what he assumed was a fashionable way. The addition to the house that extended the dining area into a sunroom at the back was done recently, presumably to increase its value for sale, and it did not escape Willie's notice that the brothers' cabin featured prominently in the pastoral view that this wing, with all its windows, had been built to highlight. George heard the construction noise, of course, but had little notion of just how the house had changed from its former quaintness to something that struck Willie as unsettlingly new and unfeasibly clean. They had been vaguely aware of the house going on the market, of people coming to see it, but they had never spoken to the realtor or to anyone else about their situation. Samson was no longer there to protect them, and Willie suspected that it would be up to the new owners whether he and his brother would be allowed to keep their small section of the world.

As they readied themselves for bed one night, Willie blurted out his worry: "I don't think we have any right to be here."

"We'll just buy the land, then," George replied, exaggerating every word and shaping each syllable carefully so that Willie could read his lips. "What else is money for?" George was having trouble understanding his brother's anxiety.

"How much have we got, exactly? And what if they don't want to sell?"

"They'll need to. What would they do with the flock if they didn't?"

"Maybe they'd hire someone new. Or sell the sheep. I bet they'd get good money. There are some top-notch ewes out there, thanks to you." Even in his moment of anxiety, Willie was still pleased with himself for the rhyme.

"Your knickers are in a twist. That's all. So let's just wait and see," said George.

Whether the arrival of the new family worried Willie more than it worried George because seeing the changes made to the property was more immediate than hearing them, the sight of time's effects more troubling than their sound, or whether the anxiety could be attributed to the elder brother's fragile temperament was an unresolved matter. Either way, Willie had been having trouble getting to sleep lately.

*

Karen spends the first morning in her new house convinced that Sally and Jackson must not find out about the shepherd situation, so in spite of the bright day, they sit in the kitchen with the lights on and the curtains closed. She absolutely does not want a repeat of the time Sally made friends with Mort, the man who slept on the bench outside the Parkdale branch of the Toronto Public Library and was given to offering her daughter paper lunch bags full of his own beard clippings. As she and the kids make pancakes, Karen feels herself relax. The bubbles start showing in the Mickey Mouse ears and Karen shakes the pan expertly, flipping the pancakes in the air before they land on their uncooked faces. Sally and Jack sit on the floor, using an opened piece of newspaper as a makeshift breakfast table, and eat as if they haven't been fed in days, gobbling up pancake after pancake until Karen has used up all the batter without having eaten anything herself. Both kids are now reading as they shovel forkfuls of pancake copiously into their mouths, chewing quietly. Jackson isn't reading a book but is completely captivated by the back of a Multigrain Cheerios box. Despite the pancakes, he'd demanded they buy cereal at the grocery store. Karen recognized the exact words she had heard her husband say before, as Jack tilted his head wisely and persuaded her: "It never goes bad. We'll be glad of it later." Karen wondered how she had produced this little boy, and bought the Cheerios.

There is a lot to do in unpacking and sorting everything out, so Karen decides to make some lists. She is sitting on the floor before she realizes that she doesn't even have a pen unpacked. Sally has begun reading her Choose-Your-Own-Adventure out loud so that Jack can make the selections.

"'You stare at the ogre before you. What do you do?'" Sally pauses dramatically and peers over the book at Jackson before offering the options. "'If you punch him in the stomach and run as fast as you can away from his cave, go to page 89. If you sing him a lullaby to try to get him to fall asleep, go to page 38.'"

"I sing!" says Jackson.

"'The ogre laughs a big belly laugh at your little song and picks you up in one of his giant hands and puts you down in his dark cave. You are now a prisoner of the evil one! The end.'" Sally whistles, a skill she has recently learned. "Sorry, Jack," she says, "want to try again?"

Karen tears open a couple of boxes labelled "Stationery" in search of a pen. She scribbles down all the things that worry her: the need for new towels, plastic liners for the kitchen cupboards, more diversions for Sally and Jack to keep them indoors until the matter is resolved. As she writes she feels increasingly capable, as though she is taking care of the tasks simply by adding loops of cursive to the notepaper. Karen finally writes a large *S* to begin the word "shepherds" as the last item on her list but immediately decides against it, leaving that single letter. Karen feels herself exhaling deeply.

"What's your deal, Sighy McSighFace?" asks Sally.

"Nothing sweetie. Just a couple of long days, don't you think? Time to run a few errands? There might be treats involved."

"You miss Dad." Jack looks up at the ceiling as he says this, as if he were witnessing a Higher Power, rather than a hanging light fixture.

"Yep, I sure do, buddy. Don't you guys?"

"Not yet," says Sally cheerfully, "but maybe I will by tomorrow. I'm interested in hearing more about those treats, though."

"Can we see the sheep for a treat?" Jackson has not given up on the idea of new pets.

"No sheep. What did I say about waiting for Dad?" Karen wonders if distracting them is actually working as well as it appears to be, and she has to concentrate hard just to sound like herself. "A loonie each for whatever you want at the Dollar Store, okay? But you have to help me get the stuff we need for the house first."

Sally extends her hand to seal the deal, and mother and daughter stand there, shaking each other's hands as if they are business acquaintances. As Sally packs her backpack with her colouring books and pencil crayons for the car, Karen feels marginally more empowered to handle the small tasks of the day, leaving the larger worry for James.

At George's insistence, the brothers keep all of their money in cash in a safe hidden under a tarp beneath his bed. Years earlier, Willie had suggested that they entrust their earnings to the bank, but George refused and the subject had never been brought up again. So there the safe remained, containing large stacks of American bills. There was some Canadian money, too, but most of what was inside was foreign currency, unusable on a day-to-day basis. Neither of the brothers had ever counted the money. They did not imagine that they were rich, nor had they any need to be. But their livelihood did depend on the well-being of that safe, so George was careful to ensure that no one except his brother knew the combination. He had the feel of the lock hardwired into him and sometimes opened it just to make sure that muscle memory wouldn't let him down in a time of need. For all his education, Willie was not very fiscally knowledgeable, although he was nebulously anxious about money, so George was the one who took care of the finances, such as they were, and opened up the safe and told Willie which bills to take out for groceries and staples.

On grocery day, George told Willie to take out an extra five dollars so they could buy one of Eliza's apple pies at the farmer's market. As they prepared for their trip, George suggested disrupting their usual ritual of travelling to the market with Travis Elcock, the buffalo farmer, at six, in order to wait and invite the newcomers along.

"Perhaps the lady wants to join us? Meet folks and see what the place has going for it?" George suggested.

"She has a car of her own," said Willie.

"It would be improper not to ask."

"Doesn't much like the look of us, George."

"No wonder, if we don't welcome her to town! I'd not like the looks of us either if we were so rude."

"Best keep quiet and not bother her."

"We have to at least introduce ourselves. It's not right."

Having agreed to stick to their usual plan on the condition that the welcome be extended later on in the day, the brothers each grab a jug of unpasteurized sheep's milk to take to the market, where they will hand it over to Jonah, who will turn it into cheese.

The market was never overwhelmingly busy, but it was the most social event of the brothers' week. There were usually about ten stalls in the parking lot outside the old grain elevator, which had recently become the local art gallery. On Saturdays, the lot was blocked off, the gallery closed, and marquees set up early for the morning's preparations. As the brothers wandered around the market, Willie admired the desultory loveliness of wooden barrels untidily overflowing with root vegetables, the mason jars full of gleaming homemade jellies, condiments, and preserves, and the drooping sweetness of wildflowers in metal buckets, a quarter a stem or a dollar for a handful. Sensory deprivation was not any more of a bother at the market than in any other situation and the brothers relied on each other to navigate the parking lot. Holding on to Willie's suspender, George shifted from foot to foot, swaying to the sound of Mr. Jenkins's harmonica and the dozens of indistinguishable voices that chattered around the stalls. When the occasional greeting leapt forth from the din, George would say hello back, and yes, he and his brother were doin' just fine thanks, a response often spoken to the horizon rather than to his interlocutor unless Willie pointed his brother in the right direction. Willie received handshakes and nods as they approached the stalls, and observed his brother's conversations to make sure everyone was comfortable. Both brothers tasted samples of plastic sticks full of cinnamon-flavoured honey, and breads, cakes, and pastries baked in someone's homemade backyard brick oven. They sipped hot apple cider from plastic cups.

Willie signalled to George when they reached Eliza's stall by tugging twice on his brother's ear, though the smell of wild blueberries and warm pastry already had George tilting his head back with pleasure. Willie waved at Eliza's sixteen-year-old daughter, Abigail, who greeted him by raising her hand shyly. The brothers' system of lip-reading for Willie and speaking back out loud for George was one that made sense to the two of them but had not been completely translated to other people (the butcher, for instance, could never get the hang of it, and was forever confusing the brothers and holding paper packages of meat out to George, expecting him to take what he couldn't see). But Eliza knew to say hello to George as she looked and nodded at Willie.

"We're having a treat this week, Liza," George said, making conversation as Willie surveyed the pies.

"Apple?"

"'Course. Unless there's a better offer?"

"Well, I've got blueberry too, and strawberry-rhubarb, but you don't like that one as much, as I remember it."

"Apple it is, sweetheart, apple it is," said George, smiling at her left shoulder.

As Eliza boxed up the pie for the brothers, Abigail helped another customer.

"Will these freeze well?" The school principal made a grand gesture to indicate the pies.

"Oh gosh. I don't know, sir. I got eight brothers so I've never seen one last more than an afternoon."

George and Eliza giggled in spite of themselves at Abigail's polite bewilderment, while Willie, wanting to know what was going on, nudged George in the ribs.

"Well, do they?" the principal asks again. "Would they be the sort of thing a man could freeze?"

Willie watched as Abigail ran her hands over her long blue skirt as though she was smoothing away her irritation.

"They sure would be," George jumped in, "and you won't regret this purchase here, sir. Best pies in town." He turned to where he thought the principal was standing, but instead faced the centre of the parking lot. Willie took George by the shoulders and, not knowing quite where to point his brother, angled him back towards Abigail. Eliza passed Willie the pie as tenderly as if she were handing over a nest full of new eggs, and he felt their hands touch as he received it.

The principal handed Abigail a bill and pivoted to face George as he waited for his blueberry pie. "Well, how are you there, George? How are those new neighbours of yours working out?"

"We don't know much yet. They just came in yesterday. Willie saw 'em getting out of their van. We wanted to give them time to settle in before we barged on up there."

"Right, well, I hear they have two kids? A boy and a girl?" The principal keeps trying. George repeats the question slowly for Willie, who says simply, "Yes." It was hard for Willie to know if he could be understood by anyone other than George, since he couldn't hear the sound of his own voice, so he frequently kept his answers brief.

"You let us know now if they give you any trouble, won't you, boys?" The principal spoke to everyone in town as though they were eleven years old.

"There's no trouble we ain't seen before, sir. I hope with these new folks we'll just keep keepin' on the way things are." George tugged Willie's ear again to signal that it was time to go. "You take care now, all of you."

The brothers ambled onward for the rest of their groceries, Willie holding on tight to the bakery box. For George, the trip to the market was all that was needed to lift the ominous mood that had descended on the property since the new tenants arrived. He fancied himself a bit of a conversationalist, and although they hadn't had much to say about the neighbours this week, they would surely be able to introduce everyone next Saturday.

In contrast, Willie felt a deepening uneasiness verging on panic throughout their morning at the market and as they rode back home in the truck. His body was reacting to the worry by sweating in places he didn't even know produced sweat, like the backs of his knees and the crooks of his elbows. Either by virtue of being a good listener, or because he knew his brother well enough to smell distress, George reached across the bench of the pickup and held Willie's hand all the way home.

*

The idea comes to Karen while she is washing the dishes. There must be some form of assisted living for retired people that would suit the shepherds. Surely there must be. Perhaps if she could arrange and even financially support their transition to a nursing home, they would be able to leave the property without too much hassle, and they would be cared for in the right ways. The more she thinks it through, the more it seems totally appropriate, the kind of thing a social worker would recommend if confronted with two frail old men attempting to make a go of it on their own in the wilderness and bothering their neighbours in the process. Standing at the sink by the window, Karen can see them now through the small gap in the curtain, hand in hand, carrying what appear to be bags of groceries back to their shack. She pulls the curtains fully shut to hide the shepherds from the kids. Fortunately, she has managed to convince Sally and Jackson to move on from their one-box police station to making a miniature Alcatraz out of the other cardboard moving boxes. As far as Karen can tell, they are as excited about the cartons as they seem to be about anything else in their new surroundings. Karen picks up the phone to share her plan with James.

"We can just get them taken care of."

"Sweetie, I think it might be a little extreme to hire a hit man." The sound of traffic obscures James's answer slightly.

"A nursing home!"

"Oh, right. Right." James seems to be eating something.

"Are you listening? I've really been thinking about this."

"Right, yeah. No, a nursing home seems good."

The audible crunching is making Karen's skin crawl, so she tells James goodbye and sits down cross-legged on a flattened box. She stares for a while at her cellphone, which still has a

Toronto number and is probably costing her a fortune. Deciding to take matters into her own hands, rather than wait for James, who might have second thoughts, she tells the children to stay where they are and goes outside to investigate the whereabouts of the shepherds. Once she sees that the coast is clear, she calls for the children, bundles them into the van, and drives to town to see if she can find someone to talk to.

When they arrive in town, she pulls up to the gas station. Karen asks the attendant, a slouchy seventeen-year-old boy, where the nursing home is as he fills the tank. The attendant's Circle K nameplate says "Jessica," presumably an example of teenage humour. He points her down the road: "Your first right, then the next left, then a right at the lights. It's at the end of that road opposite the playground."

At the word *playground*, mayhem erupts in the previously quiet back seat.

"Can we go can we go can we go?" Jackson is first to ask.

"Have you been good?"

"The best," Sally pipes in with assurance.

"Well, then, you can go. I have something to sort out first, but if you're very well behaved we can go to the playground afterwards. Deal?"

"Done deal," says Jackson.

*

The van has disappeared from the driveway by the time the brothers put away their groceries and sit down to eat their lunch of fresh sheep's cheese on hearth-baked bread. Just as they are tucking in to their second sandwiches, there is a knock at the door that gives George a fright. Both men rise to answer the door together. Waiting outside is a broad, handsome, clean-shaven man in a Ralph Lauren T-shirt.

"Hello. James Schmidt. Your new neighbour," the man says, extending a hand to George, which Willie reaches over his brother to shake.

"Pleasure to meet you, Jim," George replies. "Can we offer you some tea? Or sheep's cheese?"

"I'm fine, thanks."

"Well, I know you're fine, sir, but that doesn't really answer my question about the tea!"

Willie, noticing the awkward expression on James's face, tries to explain. "He's just bein' smart," he says, slightly too loudly.

Willie puts a pot of water on the stove to boil and serves the tea while James and George sit at the small table and begin to get to know each other. In the confusing and lengthy conversation that follows, George answers James's seemingly endless questions about the brothers and their lives.

It is hard for Willie not to feel left out as he watches the two men talk, since James keeps turning his back to him in a way that makes it impossible for Willie to see what he is saying. Every so often Willie attempts to add something, only to discover that he has missed a crucial part of the conversation. Eventually he stops trying and sits on his own bed, sipping sullenly at his tea as if it tastes vile.

By the end of the half-hour conversation, which covers the brothers' life in Texas, their work with the sheep, their family, their ages, marital statuses (as if these were really in question), and their health, George is half-slumped over with fatigue, resting his chin on his palm, and Willie is so anxious he can hardly sit still.

"We like to stay thinking about the present moment, sir, not worry too much about what's done already. But I can tell you Samson was very good to us, and then his son was after him, and we did well by that family and we'd be very happy to do right by you and your wife and the little ones." George's voice is soft, almost meditative, but he is worrying his fingers in and out of his belt loops as he speaks. "We take or leave people as they come, Jim, that's how we do it."

When James finally leaves, it is with a courteous "pleasure to meet you" for George, and a handshake and nod for Willie. Once the door closes behind him, the brothers sit on their respective beds. Their bodies are curved towards each other. For a few minutes they are motionless, taking it all in. Finally, Willie reaches across to place a hand on his brother's knee instead of asking the question directly.

"All we can do," says George, resting his hand on top of his brother's, "is hold our breath for what's to come."

When Karen and the kids arrive home just as the sky is beginning to soften into evening, James greets her at the door, and they kiss for a long time. Karen can hardly bring herself to stop until Sally begins to make disgusted sounds and pretends to throw up.

"I didn't know you were getting an earlier connection."

"I went down to meet the gentlemen while you were out."

"We went to investigate the nursing home. They've been trying for a while, apparently, to get the brothers to move there but they won't leave. The nurse said that if I could manage to persuade them, the home would definitely be willing to take them in."

"We played on the swings!" Jackson interjects.

"Good, buddy!" James picks Jackson up, tosses him nonchalantly over his shoulder and then cranes his neck so he can see his wife. "Aren't you at all curious to know what they're like? They mentioned that you hadn't introduced yourself."

"Who are we talking about, exactly?" Sally starts looking around, as if there are aged strangers hiding in the mudroom. "I'm still confused about why I had to play piano for all those old people. I don't think I'll like it here if I have to do that when we do chores."

"It's like I told you," says Karen, "we're getting to know people in the new town." She can hear that her own voice sounds less certain now that she's been cracked open by James's arrival, but she keeps trying. "Don't worry about it, Sally. Daddy and I will talk about this later." She leans in towards her husband and runs her hand along his free arm.

"I guess. I think it might be healthier to have friends my own age, though. That's what you said about Mort, and he was way more awesome than the old ladies today who just sat there and dribbled."

"Can we play outside now?" asks Jackson, jumping down from his perch.

Karen says *no* and James says *yes* at exactly the same time. The kids stand still for a moment and then start to go, assuming that this will satisfy both parties. As they rush out the door, Karen opens her mouth to tell them to stop, but then thinks better of it. Instead, she walks into the kitchen and pulls back the curtains for the first time since they arrived. She sees Sally and Jackson careen towards the sheep, who seem to be yodelling with confusion and are beginning to back away from the fence and from her hooligan children. She turns back to James.

"I guess it has to happen sometime," she says, "but if this is a disaster it's your fault."

"They're all right." He pulls her close.

She is not sure whether he means the shepherds or the kids, but she sinks into her husband, and closes her eyes briefly. Then she lifts her head and looks to him, seeking an answer.

"So, what did they say? Will they go?"

IT TASTES WONDERFUL

☞ "WHAT? WHAT DO YOU WANT FROM ME?" Jay stands in front of the 24-hour supermarket, loosening his tie and picking a fight with the moon. It's almost midnight and the super-moon is in full glow. He knows that's not its scientific name, but it's the term he's heard everyone using. It looms so close to the city these days you can see every shadow on its pocked surface. Jay is having an unexpected reaction to this augmented lunar presence, which seems to have careened out of its orbit and started invading his personal space. It makes him uncomfortable, like the moon is a sweaty dude pressed up into him on the subway.

Jay is shaking his fist at the heavens when a screeching noise alerts him to the fact that he's standing close enough to the supermarket's entrance to set off the automatic door, making it open and close, open and close. Now the alarm is sounding. He steps forward and lets the door do its thing and shut behind him. Inside, the 24-hour MegaFresh is fluoride-bright and ultra happy, and Jay needs a minute to adjust to this raw light after the clammy glow of the moon. He rests his briefcase beside the stack of baskets by the door and closes his eyes, then opens them to the sharp white-blue. Everywhere in the supermarket are little yellow signs exclaiming the most ordinary things. Apples! $0.63 each! JUMBO Bran Flakes! $5.76 a box! And what he was on his way to pick up when the celestial body got all up in his business: Coffee!

His girlfriend can't get out of bed without her caffeine hit. Every morning he places a cup on her bedside table before he heads to the office, leaving the coffee to go cold as she dozes. He's never asked Lisa if she drinks it like that or if she warms it up, but he knows she loves it when he brings her coffee in bed. Or at least she used to. When he and Lisa were first going out, almost eight years ago now, she introduced him to her dance company not as her boyfriend but as her "coffee provider." He wasn't sure, even then, whether to be offended or pleased, but he loved having his arm around her small waist the way he did in that moment, so he just held tight. "This one's a keeper," her choreographer enthused. "He is," Lisa confirmed, secretly pinching his ass. "He totally is." So it doesn't matter if she drinks the coffee or not. What matters is that he keeps up his end of the deal.

The best thing about being someone's main squeeze and living in Toronto, in Jay's opinion, is that it's a city where there's always a supermarket open, even if it seems too late. Tonight, Jay almost has MegaFresh to himself. The night manager and the punk cashier are playing cards in the 10-items-or-less aisle. There's a new mum, her belly still soft with the trace of what she's carried, strolling her fussy baby up and down the frozen meat section. Jay wishes he could empty out the store completely so that he could joy ride on the carts the way he used to as a teenager in Superstore parking lots. While his parents were busy at the checkout, he'd step up onto the back of a cart, push off with one foot, lean forward on the handlebar, and ride down the concrete ramp like it had no end. It was best when no one was watching. But he never gets the chance to ride free like that now. Even this late at night, he's never managed to be totally alone.

Lisa and Jay once loved each other. Jay doesn't think about it in these terms very often, but it has been five and a half months since they had sex (a brief, middle-of-the-night, half-pajamaed fumble that Jay almost mistook for a dream), and three months and seven days since their last kiss (a peck on the cheek at a friend's engagement party). These days, he avoids thinking about sex at all unless he is alone in the shower with the fan on and the door closed. Jay tries not to dwell on this. Instead, he follows the mum, who has a small glob of something that looks like toothpaste stuck to the strands of her ponytail, as she moves on to Tea! Coffee! Condiments! Jay picks up two packages of espresso and compares the medium roast to the dark, testing their weight in his hands, which in each case is exactly 500 grams, according to the labels.

Jay has been spending a lot of time at the gym. He can now Olympic lift more than he even knew it was possible for a person to hold on his own, and he has come to love the treadmill, and the long, slow warmth in his quads and hamstrings as he works up a hill, the heart-rate monitor he wears strapped to his chest that tells him how hard and how long and how far he should go. Even his face has stronger edges now. It is as though his old features have melted away, and underneath he found the cheekbones and jawline of the kind of man his advertising firm would cast in a campaign for an expensive, smoky Scotch. If only he had learned to depend on the sensation of pushing and burning and pleasantly hurting as a teenager, he sometimes thinks, rather than only in his forties, perhaps he would now be an altogether different man.

Despite his year-long transformation, Lisa hasn't said anything about the change. The other day, on her way out the door, she put a hand on his stomach and patted it in a familiar almost platonic way, as though the six-pack had always been there. She has said nothing about his new wardrobe, and when he spent over two thousand dollars on clothes on the shared credit card last month, she just paid the bill without comment.

A noisy prattle of cans hitting the floor startles Jay out of his daze. He turns in the direction of the noise and finds the MegaFresh manager rebuilding the coconut milk display he just knocked over. The mother and her baby have moved on. He is still clutching a pack of coffee in each hand, and when he looks at his watch he realizes he's been standing there for almost fifteen minutes. He picks the dark roast, as usual.

So how does a person come to be buying ground coffee for a woman who no longer loves him late on a Tuesday night? He and Lisa are not married. They have no children. He could leave whenever he wants. Sometimes, as he's drying dishes that haven't been properly washed, or scrubbing the bathroom floor, he imagines skipping town and then tries to imagine her crying, or calling her friend Sophia from the studio, cradling the cell phone between her shoulder and her cheek and hugging her own body. But try as he might to conjure a vision of her curled up in the fetal position on their carpet, listening to Joni Mitchell, it's never truly her. It's always someone else in Lisa's clothing. It seems more realistic to picture her rolling over in bed and going back to sleep, the way she does every morning after he places her coffee on her nightstand. When he imagines that scene, it is Lisa's shape that curves back into the duvet; it's Lisa's arm that falls elegantly across his side of the bed. He's fantasized about telling her he's leaving just as she emerges from the bath, dripping wet and clean, while he stands there in one of his new suits, holding his single, carefully packed briefcase. But even in this scenario, she reacts to his news by flipping her dark hair over and wrapping it up in a towel, before wandering out to the living room to slouch on the couch in front of the TV.

Sometimes Jay stands in his living room when Lisa isn't home and pretends he's being interviewed about his Great Escape. "Yes," he says to the broom handle, "it was a tough call. She's a beautiful lady . . . My getaway was such a powerful experience. In fact, you might just say everything in my life was leading up to that horse with an empty saddle pulling up in front of our condo building. The steed just said to me, 'Jay, welcome to travel by horse. It is wonderful and free and solitary. You will love it, and I've saved my saddle just for you.' . . . No, no, I don't talk to horses. It was a figure of speech. People say that, don't they, that things 'called out to them'?" Jay always ends these imaginary interviews by laughing self-deprecatingly and staring at the carpet, suddenly self-conscious, even though there is no Lisa there to judge him.

Of course these are only musings, because he can't imagine learning a whole new way of living that doesn't include her. While it's easy to see Lisa on her own, eating Bran Flakes! at their kitchen counter as though nothing has changed, he can't see himself going on in the same way. He has never lived with anyone else, nor has he ever lived alone, so it seems simply impossible. And anyway, he doesn't actually want to go. So he always clears his throat at the end of his reveries and carries on with the housework. But sometimes the empty apartment makes him brave enough to think about starting over.

Jay wanders up the Toiletries! Housewares! Cleaning Products! aisle of MegaFresh, coffee in hand, and stops in front of the shampoo and conditioner section. He flips open a manly-looking blue bottle of 2-in-1 and smells it. The scent is noxious and wrong, like aftershave laced with gasoline. Too manly, maybe. He pops the lid on another and inhales slowly. This one has notes of citrus, a "pleasantly acidic nose," as Lisa would say. She took a wine tasting course with her friend Blake last summer, and now insists on using the lingo, describing a Shiraz the way Jay himself might describe a pirate – "big," "aggressive," "blowsy." Jay doesn't know the difference between "earthy" and "fleshy" wines, but if Lisa had asked him to come along, he would have happily swirled and smelled and drank the stuff before bickering gently with her about the "mouth-feel" of the grape. "Zingy" and "refreshing" is how the bottle describes the conditioner in his hand. Now those are good adjectives, Jay thinks. It's hard to turn off his professional eye. He has been in the business of branding long enough now that nearly everything he sees becomes a commodity in need of a sales pitch. MegaFresh's own particular strategy is to make everything seem thrilling! And Jay feels it. He does! It makes him want to buy more out of sheer professional admiration. He tucks the bottle under his arm and leaves the aisle, deliberately avoiding the leave-in conditioners.

About eight months ago, just after Lisa started to dance less and organize more, working full-time to manage the studio, Jay started to apply excessive amounts of her leave-in conditioner to his hair. It began with an accident. He knocked the bottle off the shower caddy and the lid fell off. He was about to put it back, but instead he found himself following the directions on the bottle slavishly, except he just used more. He started at the roots, as the bottle recommended, and he sprayed and sprayed until his hair was wet through. Then he used it on the hair on the other parts of his body. He rubbed it in circular motions onto his chest, lingering at the nipples. The stuff smelled vaguely like marijuana with a soft, enduring hint of coconut, and there was something in the fine print about herbs and botanicals. It also smelled like her in a way she wouldn't notice, but that caught him every so often when he tucked her hair away to kiss her cheek.

Lisa never remarked on his new hair, always slick with product. She just let Jay touch the back of his hand to her face as though he was testing for a fever and say something about how her skin was as perfect as a ripe peach. "You're sweet," she'd say, her eyes fixed on the TV as he ran his hand over her shoulder and down her arm, where he let it rest, hardly touching her. Jay was going through more than one bottle a month, stealthily replacing it in Lisa's absence, hoping she wouldn't notice the extra expenditure. It was pricey stuff. Looked fancy, too, in its silver bottle with *silky* in cursive lettering. He thought about switching to a drugstore brand for himself, and leaving Lisa to her outrageously expensive but sparingly applied conditioner, but he figured it would be better to kick the habit altogether than to risk trying something new.

Jay runs an open hand over his hair. He's finding it easy to get distracted by all the things he could bring home. He wanders over to the baking aisle to see if they've restocked the Tahitian vanilla beans Lisa likes to put in her shortbread. She never eats the cookies herself, so he's her taste tester. "Trying to quit!" she'd say brightly if Jay ever suggests that she have one, though it wasn't a habit she'd ever had in the first place, as far as he knew. When he asked her why she spent all that time baking cookies no dancer would even think of eating, she'd just wipe her hands on a dishtowel and say, "It's the quickest way to make something out of nothing. I put all the right measurements of the right ingredients in and it just works every time. And plus, you love them, right?" She knew he did. That's why she used to leave two cookies on a plate for him by the espresso machine for when he got home from work. She hasn't procrasti-baked in a long time, not since she started teaching ballet to four-year-olds on weekend afternoons and hanging out with the other instructors afterwards, staying out late for dinner and drinks. She has also stopped sorting their mail, including the flyers and coupons, by colour – a useless organizational tactic that began five years ago as a joke about Jay's overly fastidious filing systems. Now the mail just sits on the counter in a large unsorted pile, and the apartment smells like conditioner instead of vanilla.

"I'm really busy with work right now," she texted him last week when he had asked if she'd be home for dinner. And a minute later: "You of all people should understand that."

"I'm just asking," Jay texted back, "if you want me to get some food ready."

"Nothing for me. Don't wait up."

"OK," Jay texted, and paused for a moment before adding a kiss.

Lately, Jay finds it easier to talk to her while she sleeps. Sometimes she murmurs gorgeous nonsense in response. Other times she even mumbles affection. "You're too sweet," she said the other night when he was encouraging her, praising each of her eyelashes and tracing his finger around the curl of her ear.

Jay hopes that she might not be able to resist the lure of the new beans. But the supermarket is still out of stock.

When Jay begins to tire of browsing shelf after shelf of smartly packaged food and daydreaming about his own daydreams, he makes his way to the only open checkout counter. In front of him is a man who, although he appears to be in his thirties, is wearing a tweed cap and a sweater vest under a blazer with a pocket square. On someone else the ensemble might have seemed dapper – trendy, even – but the man's clothes are loose and ill-fitting and highlight his scrawny frame. He has inky, bluish-black marks on his temples and his eyes dart furtively beneath bushy eyebrows. He reminds Jay of one of the guys from Lisa's dance program at NYU: slightly affected and a little dirty, as if one day he decided what he would look like every day for the rest of his life, cobwebs and hair growth notwithstanding. Jay runs his hand down the front of his suit jacket and removes a reusable shopping bag from his briefcase as he gets in line behind the somewhat unsettling man.

"I already had chicken today, but I didn't have any bread," the man says, staring past Jay, probably at the display of plastic lemons filled with lemon juice, or at the pyramid of actual lemons beside it. "You're not buying any chicken. Not overly fond of the bird?"

"Oh, I like chickens okay," Jay says, in case the stranger is talking to him.

"However, I don't make a habit of eating chicken wings," the man says, staring up at the ceiling now and blinking hard at the ruthless lights. "There are bones from all different birds and that's not healthy. Different parts of different chickens. That is not good for your heart. Wouldn't you agree?"

As Jay offers a weak nod, a twitch crumples the man's face every few seconds, like a newspaper that's been thrown into a campfire.

"The best thing you can do for your heart is to stay outdoors," the man continues. "I ride my bicycle every day. Will you look at that?" He pulls a quarter from his breast pocket and examines it. "It's a silver quarter. Real silver. You know, the Canadian mint produced genuine silver quarters until 1967, and then they switched to aluminum. I'll just keep this right here next to my heart. It's very important to take care of your ticker. I personally have a strong heart –"

"That'll be three eighty-nine, sir," the punk cashier says once she rings his bread through.

"Oh, I see. I see now. Well, that's very expensive."

"Yes, sir."

"Well, I need some bread, don't I?"

"I've rung it through now."

"I have a strong heart, you know, and I've already eaten some chicken today. Actually, I also tried to eat a fruit from the Chinese market. As a matter of fact, it was very expensive, too. It was brown and it was like a flower, but when I bit into it, well, that was a painful experience. Yes, the husk was hard, but a beautiful juice emerged from the centre, a milky white juice from the middle of the flower, and that tasted delicious. It tasted wonderful. I had hoped you could eat the whole thing, though, because those are expensive fruits. You can only get them at the Chinese market in the summer."

Jay considers saying the word *lychee* to give the man's poetic description a name. For some reason, he doesn't. He understands the feeling, though. Once in a while you put something in your mouth that tastes exquisite. Not just the usual kind of nice, or tasty, like when your sister makes Thanksgiving dinner for the family and everyone says, "Well, isn't this delicious!" And it is. But it doesn't take you to that next level, that place beyond delectable that makes your whole mouth and heart and stomach turn luscious, turn meltingly into gold. Jay is quite sure this is the feeling the man is talking about, only Jay wouldn't get it from lychees. He thinks fleetingly of his new shampoo, of massaging it in a circular motion through his hair, of the water running down his neck. To each his own. But instead of agreeing, instead of saying, "Yes, you've totally got it! Tell everyone about exceptional fruit!", he watches as the man declines a plastic bag, picks up the bread, and tips his cap. "Keep the change," Jay says as he pays for his own groceries in a rush and follows him outside, where he watches from a safe distance as the man hops onto his bicycle – the plastic bag of bread dangling from the handlebars – and teeters away.

Jay pauses for a minute by the bike racks. Wedged between an orange hipster bike with a wicker basket and a fancy new road bike with impossibly thin tires is a teal beater. It's rusted in the body and has a kickstand that sticks out from its socket like a badly broken bone. There's a U-shaped lock fixed to a clip on the back wheel, but it's not attached to the rack. It's no shopping cart in an empty supermarket, but it's the next best thing. He looks around to see if anyone's watching: an elderly woman wearing at least four layers of clothing sleeps beside the drug store across the street. There's no one else around. Instead of walking in the direction of his condo, he puts his grocery bag into the basket at the front of the bike, balances his briefcase precariously on top, and grips the handbrakes to make sure they work. So far, so good. He backs the bike out, steps up on the pedals, and begins to ride away. The bike is too small and his knees nearly hit the handlebars with each turn of the pedals, but he rides faster anyway. Though he pounds away on the high-tech recumbent exercise bikes at the gym, he hasn't ridden an actual bike since he was a child. It's been at least three decades since he's pushed himself forward with his own strength, but it's true what they say about never forgetting. Barrelling through the city streets without a helmet, one hand on the handlebar, he picks up so much speed that his eyes water and his breath quickens. By the time he's travelled five blocks he finds his rhythm and air is gathering in his sleeves. The world seems quieter than usual, but his own body sounds louder: there's wind billowing inside his ears like he's listening to the sea.

He cycles down to the lakeshore and, having cleared the clutter of city light, he turns towards the water and rides head-on into the wind. There's the stupid moon again, now that it's come out from hiding behind a condo building. It's so big that the sky is bright to bursting. Who does the moon think he is?

Jay can feel his suit pants rubbing against the seat of the bike, and his tie needs further loosening, but he pedals on, the bike now bouncing along the wooden boardwalk beside the open water. At the end of the path, he rides into the empty concrete stretch of parking lot beside the entrance to the Canadian National Exhibition grounds, with its grand archway topped by the winged stone angel who guards the nation's miniature ponies and corn on the cob. Our Lady of the Midway. Jay breathes in diaphragm-deep before he leans back in a way he hasn't done since he was ten and pulls a wheelie. As he tugs on the handlebars he can feel the weight of the bike lift off the ground, and he rises – not quite up, and not quite away, just a little higher than in everyday life. The trick doesn't last long. As the front wheel drops jerkily back onto the ground, a siren cuts through the quiet spectacle of his only show-off move. He starts to hear the world again as the front wheel strikes the pavement a second time. For a moment he is simply astonished that he hasn't fallen. As he turns the pedals in a slower, smoother motion, keeping himself steady, his throat tightens at the thought that he's stolen this bike – even if only for a short ride. What would Lisa say if she saw him now, moon-crazed and loose-tied, riding a stolen bike as proudly as a kid with training wheels? He loops the bike in a wide circle around the lot and turns in the direction of home.

Jay rides, slower now, through the side streets full of shambling Victorian houses, their gardens trellised with still-green cherry tomatoes. As he pauses at a stop sign, despite there being no cars around, he's reminded of the elderly man who used to ride his bike along the same route past their condo every day whistling show tunes. He has never seen anyone be as consistently cheerful as the musical cyclist in his reflective clothing and trouser clips. Jay and Lisa used to call each other to the window whenever The Whistler passed by, waving at him from the seventh floor, even though he never noticed them, but it's been months since they've had reason to do so. Even though Jay has kept watch, the poor guy hasn't been around lately. Lisa thinks that The Whistler is old enough to have died, but Jay hopes that he has just moved to a seniors' community where bicycle riding is encouraged.

The uncompromisingly chipper glow of the MegaFresh sign welcomes him back to his neighbourhood. Stepping off the bike, Jay pretends not to notice that the punk cashier is standing outside smoking and no doubt watching him as he rests the bike back up against the stand. He almost expects her to unleash her inner black belt and charge towards him howling Tarzan-style while she delivers a flying kick right to his chest. "Honestly," she'd say, keeping him pinned to the ground with her foot on his sternum until the cops arrived and gave him the right to remain silent, "why would someone like you need to take what isn't yours?" But the girl tosses her cigarette on the ground and turns to go back into the store. Instead of relief, Jay feels as if she does have her foot firmly planted in the centre of his chest. She tossed his grand performance away so easily: the butt-end of a slow day.

When he arrives home, the condo is dark and smells of laundry detergent. It's Clean Breeze, a scent designed to give clothes the impression of lightness and fresh air. Still, Jay can't help himself from breathing in deeply. He sets his briefcase down by the door and navigates by the moon's soft light to the kitchen to ready the coffee for the morning. He opens up the espresso and fills the chamber of the coffee grinder so that all he has to do when he wakes up is hit "start." There is nothing on the counter except an unsorted pile of mail.

Maybe he's been unfair to the moon, which is still enormous outside the living room window. Actually, now that he really looks, it seems to have backed off a little. Jay can't say why, but he just needs the moon to be the right size. What if the lunatic became so narcissistic it stopped knowing when to pull the waves in? Maybe it's already forgotten its role in the ordinary pull and push of days. That might explain why Jay has fallen out of his usual rhythms lately: he can't predict when he'll want to rush home and when he'll feel so far away from her he can hardly remember why he's there at all. Or maybe there are no cycles left to follow, no steady movement of days into nights into days. With a conciliatory nod at the moon, Jay closes the curtains and gets ready for bed. He doesn't turn on the bedroom light for fear of waking Lisa, so he puts his T-shirt on backwards and feels the tag scratching his neck as he lies down next to her and rests his cheek against her shoulder. She shrugs him off and murmurs, but doesn't wake. He turns his back to her, draws his knees in close to his chest, and closes his eyes.

After what feels like hours, but, according to the alarm clock, is only ten minutes of insomnia, he rolls over and strokes Lisa's back. He wants to tell her about stealing the bike, about riding it down to the CNE as if he were racing in the Tour de France. But it seems too important to share, too personal even to whisper – eye-watering wind and the lift of that wheel off the ground, his body fully aware of itself, belonging only to him. Instead, he describes the man at the store. "You remember Rick from NYU?" "Nnnhmmm," she says, with a little twitch of her lovely hand on top of the sheets. He lowers his voice even more: "The guy at the store was like him, but even more peculiar. You'd know what I mean if you saw him." Lisa's breath is slow and smooth. Jay stops moving his hand and rests the whole of his palm on the curve of her back. "I just want to know if you still . . . ," he starts, but can't finish. "Actually, I don't. You don't have to answer." When she responds by snuffling unintelligibly, he kisses her shoulder through her pajamas.

He rests there beside her for a moment and then sits up, swings his legs over the edge of the bed, and fixes his feet on the ground. He walks through the dark and opens the door, turning the handle slowly so the latch makes no sound. In the empty living room, he turns on the light and begins to do sit-ups in his T-shirt and boxer shorts. He switches to push-ups, straightening himself out into a plank. He braces himself there for a moment before lowering his chest to the ground and then rising up again, repeating the movement over and over, each one the same as the last. He works out until there is sweat dripping onto the carpet and his core starts to tremble as a warm ache pulls across his chest and blooms in his arms. He knows he should go to bed, should try to sleep, should try to get back into a steady rhythm, but somehow he can't bring himself to stop. Right now, this is the best thing he can do for his heart.

QUITE EVERYDAY LOOKING

☞ THE TRIP WAS BOTH MORE AND LESS THAN Edna Crawford had imagined it would be. The Big Apple itself had been uninspiring, which was a surprise, because she thought she was so well prepared. After all, she and Calvin read the *New York Times* every day. She couldn't help her postcard-glossy expectations: the rousing swing of the Wonder Wheel's unsteady seats at Coney Island; the popping of her ears during the elevator ride to the top of the Empire State Building. The Travel section has been Edna's favourite part of the paper since they started a family, and she could easily spend hours reading about the beaches of Belize and the tortoises of the Galapagos, mapping out fantasy itineraries. She always stayed up late after the girls had gone to bed, occupying the time before Calvin got home from the restaurant by costing out hotels online and reading traveller reviews, as though they would be able to afford the time and money to go.

New York was their first real vacation together since their oldest, Emma, was born twelve years ago. Sure, there had been summer cottage stays and campground weekends, but they hadn't been outside the drivable Pacific Northwest and they always brought the girls. Edna couldn't wait to take a vacation that didn't involve water slides and Flintstones-themed adventure playgrounds. She expected it would be tricky to pick a destination when the time came, but she surprised herself by being decisive. She had full itineraries ready for Paris, London, and Tokyo. They could have breathed the lavender air in Provence, or joined an Alaskan cruise. This year, though, she had in her grade eleven class a new student from Brooklyn whose accent was full sun against the temperate West Coast drizzle the rest of them spoke. His way of talking marked him not as an outsider, but as the king of the teenagers. He was only fourteen, but he had known what it meant to live at the centre of the world, rather than on the edge of the sea, on a wobbly tectonic plate that was always threatening to slide into the Pacific. Edna took his arrival in her class as a sign.

"New York," she'd replied when Calvin asked where they should go.

"I think that might be the most definite choice you've ever made," he said, elbowing her gently, and teasing, "Don't I get a say?"

"Nope. That's what I want."

"Then that's where we'll go." Calvin gave her a noogie, rubbing the top of her head with his knuckles the way he would do to one of the girls. Clearly, they needed some time to themselves.

They arranged to leave Emma and Liz with her sister for the week. The girls came to the airport to see them off.

"Can you get me a Yankees jersey?" asked Emma, who was the star pitcher on her little league softball team.

"Consider it done," said Calvin. Too quick as usual with his promises, as far as Edna was concerned. Those shirts are expensive.

"We'll see," she said, wanting to avoid false hopes, "but we'll bring you both back something nice." She kissed Liz's cheek. "What do you want, Lizzie?"

"A hug," said Liz.

Calvin picked her up and swung her around in such a wide circle that she stumbled and put her hands to her dizzy head when he set her back down. "Right, kiddos. We're off!"

Though Liz was struggling not to cry, Emma waved exuberantly at them and held her little sister's hand as Edna and Calvin waved back from the security lineup.

As they boarded the plane, Edna felt defiant about having left her saggy one-piece swimsuit behind in her underwear drawer so she could bring her only negligée: a red, semi-transparent lace number. Throwing it in her suitcase was an optimistic gesture, since she almost certainly wouldn't be able to close the hooks and eyes now; even so, its presence in her impeccably packed luggage was a small triumph. She pictured the two of them frequenting Art Deco cocktail bars – her in a fur shrug and a shapely black gown and him in a suit – holding each other passionately by the elbows like a couple in the movies. The New York version of her was slim, with bare, smooth legs rather than thick, sturdy calves in support socks. And surely as soon as the plane touched down at JFK, she would instantly know how to apply liquid eyeliner precisely and her hair would emerge in elegant finger waves when she lifted her head from the neck pillow. Once they arrived in the metropolis, she and Calvin would weave as naturally as shoaling fish through the crowds of glimmering bodies, darting and disappearing in the multitude.

As it turned out, the real New York was oddly quiet. Of all the things she thought it would be, she hadn't imagined the modesty, the general ordinariness. Regular trees, empty sidewalks, average-sized dumpsters with normal amounts of garbage. Even the Statue of Liberty was smaller than she had imagined. And Calvin had laughed at her for that, for thinking it small when it was clearly colossal. He quoted from the guidebook, which claimed that it measured 111 feet from the heel to the top of the head. "Think about it," he said. "I'm just over six feet, and that's pretty tall for a real human being. She's massive." Then he leaned his head back, his eyes tilted up to her crown. Still, Edna felt that there was something underwhelming about poor Liberty.

Even Macy's had been a disappointment. All the empty clothes came in size Triple Extra-Large. The whole place was picked over, just as insipid as the rest of the city. Lonely. Not only because of what happened six days into their holiday, but in a broad, atmospheric way.

Sitting in the airport, waiting for the plane to take her home, Edna lets herself think, again, about whether she could have changed anything. If she had paused just for a second, had waited for him rather than walking on. If she had given them more breathing room between Central Park and cocktails. She stops herself and tries to think about something else. No use regretting or worrying, right? Because those things don't alter the landscape. You can only do what you can do, as Calvin liked to say. Worry is useless. It's like wool that won't knit up right. It's like wool without knitting needles. She still doesn't understand why knitting needles are no longer allowed on planes. If they were, she would have something to occupy her hands right now: the fan-lace scarf she's working on for Liz. Who doesn't know yet. She's picked up the phone in the hotel room several times in the past few days and each time she's put it down again without dialling. Because . . . how? How will she say what she has to say? When she tries to phrase it in her head it comes out in spools of yarn instead of words, looping and tangling and folding in on themselves. What if everything stayed woolly? If she says nothing about it out loud, has it really happened? To distract herself, she starts clicking the end of her pen and watches the ballpoint poke in and out, in and out of the plastic shell. That would have driven Calvin crazy. But surely the pen was just as dangerous as a knitting needle? If ever the need arose you could poke a pen into all sorts of vulnerable places, someone's eye or neck for instance, and you could do a lot of damage. Edna wouldn't hesitate to protect herself, now that she was on her own. She might be from Victoria, where a stranger was more likely to open a door for you or give you a pat on the back than attack you, but she knew that much about the wide world. No use worrying about what you would do if someone harasses you. Make a plan. Have a pen handy. There are all kinds of everyday-looking things that can be used for violence if necessary. That's not worry. That's action. It's been a long, long time since she's had to worry about her own safety.

If only she was knitting right now, rather than trying to figure out sudoku, having finished the last crossword in Calvin's abandoned book of puzzles. The status of her plane on the departures board continues to say "Delayed" in glowing red letters, with no indication of when this delay will end.

Edna and Calvin met in university. He sat next to her in first-year Calculus and copied all her answers. They kissed at a dorm party and then Edna got bashful, so they didn't start dating until several weeks later, when he showed up unannounced at her shared dorm room and declared his intention to marry her someday. He dropped out the following year, and moved from job to job until he enrolled in culinary school, where he didn't have to copy his fellow students. Edna would come home to plastic buckets overflowing with slivered onions when he was practising knife skills, and even, on one occasion, to a whole pig sectioned into its tastiest cuts, the trotters cleaned and bubbling into gelatin on the stove. It suited him: buzzing around the kitchen, stirring, flipping, and poking the sizzling delights, then plating tenderly with his hands. Edna almost never cooked. The most she ever made was toast. But instead of the usual clumsy homemade sandwiches, the girls were brought up on duck confit and day-old baguettes from the restaurant.

His main interest, New York–wise, was the food. Normally, they almost never ate out, but they splurged on a fancy meal at a restaurant he'd chosen on the first night. This was his only contribution to the planning of the trip. Edna ordered a spot-prawn risotto and then white wine–poached pears in star anise for dessert, and the meal was so delicate and finely flavoured she was practically floating above their dining table. The only other time she remembered feeling as though she were levitating was when she shimmied exuberantly into the second hour of a Zumba class and the endorphins made everything shiny. Calvin was less impressed with his poussin and his chocolate fondant, but that was the attitude he took towards all meals he hadn't made himself, so Edna knew not to trust the dismissive arch of his eyebrow. The chocolate probably tasted super-nova fabulous. She suspected this was the case because he hadn't offered her a single bite. Her meal that evening was the only thing about New York that hadn't let her down.

In the airport lounge, Edna sits opposite a family of four and a small lost bird. The little boy of the family, who looks to be about five years old, keeps his eyes on the sparrow as it hops along the carpet.

"I wonder how it got in here," his teenaged sister says, watching the bird as she untangles the cord from her earphones. "Fucking depths of the building, et cetera."

"Leave it alone, Alec." Their mother has been staring at the same page of her magazine for the last hour and tapping her foot like a madwoman, occasionally glaring at their father, who is stretched out across four chairs beside them, napping. "And you," she says, without looking at her daughter, "can watch your mouth. Last thing we need right now is a hassle."

The daughter gestures rudely at her mother and puts one earphone into her ear.

"Do birds die if they can't be outside?" Alec is now tapping his foot rapidly as he warbles his concern.

"*I* am going to die if we have to stay here much longer." The girl puts in her other earphone and starts head banging theatrically to music that Edna cannot imagine. For the next few minutes, she can't help herself from staring as the girl's shoulder-length hair swishes around in the recirculated air, obscuring her face. Once it is clear that her mother is sufficiently irritated but unlikely to outwardly react in any strong way, the girl combs her hands through her hair and ends her private party. She slips off her sneakers and sits cross-legged, tucking her knees under the awkwardly placed armrests. Closes her eyes like a yogi.

Edna has seen this girl before. Dozens of her. She has seen every conceivable version of this girl over the years in her classes. Hard to tell if she will snap out of her rudeness eventually, or if she will remain spoiled. She's exactly the kind of girl who would make Emma feel stocky and unbeautiful once the earthquake of adolescence struck. Who would tease her at school for wearing jerseys, for failing to comb her hair. But Emma would be okay. Liz, too.

When Edna and Calvin left the hotel on the sixth morning of their trip, they didn't have an itinerary for the day. Edna had wanted, at first, to pack the vacation full of sightseeing, to take it all in and really get the most out of their ten days in the city. She purchased three guidebooks and had been reading selections aloud to him for weeks before they left. She'd marked relevant pages with Post-it notes, and drawn up daily schedules.

"Once a teacher, always a teacher," Calvin said, flicking a pink Post-it in the Attractions section.

"Oh, shush. If it was up to you, we'd aimlessly wander the streets for ten days, stopping only for gourmet donuts."

The museums were open earliest, so they started their days with dinosaurs at the Natural History Museum or hideous abstract paintings at the Guggenheim before taking a pre-planned scenic route to their next destination. She'd spent hours on Internet forums seeking out-of-the-way cafés where the locals ate. With all her energy focused on one place, rather than the travel offerings of the entire world, she came up with more things to see and do than they could possibly have managed in ten days.

They were snuggling against the wind on the ferry coming back from Ellis Island – Edna reading aloud from the guidebook's section on the history of immigration – when Calvin tucked a stray lock of hair behind her ear and said, "Listen, honey. I enjoyed sprinting from the subway to the terminal to catch the boat, especially when you elbowed that old guy on his walker out of the way" – he paused to kiss her forehead – "but I'm not sure you're getting the hang of taking a break. What if tomorrow we just took it a little slower, eh?"

So, instead of lining up outside the MoMa, they went in search of authentic New York bagels for their breakfast. This way they could be both touristy and relaxed: a compromise, said Calvin. At first, spending a couple of hours in the morning reading the paper and drinking coffee just as they would have done at home seemed a waste. But Edna's breathing soon became deep and full again, and she could tell by the softening of his squint that Calvin was relieved to have a break from traipsing around museums. Somehow the disappointing gentleness of what was supposed to be the most exciting city in the world bothered her less once they were back to their regular routine.

"What can I getcha?" The waitress had the upright posture of a ballerina, and she held her pencil above her ticket with a delicate arch of her wrist.

"Two New York bagels and two coffees, please," Calvin said.

"You can just call them bagels, hon, but sure thing! Cream or milk or sugar for the coffees?" Her lips were watermelon-pink and shimmery.

"Milk and sugar, thank you."

"Your accent is super-adorable! You from Minnesota?"

"Canada, actually," said Calvin, meeting her gaze and then letting his eyes wander.

The waitress laughed. "Awesome! America's hat, my dad calls it." She paused for a moment and her perfectly smooth forehead furrowed. "Is that offensive? I don't mean it like that. I love Canadians!"

"That's okay," said Calvin, and then with the first real enthusiasm Edna had heard him muster on the trip: "We love New Yorkers!"

The waitress hadn't looked at her at all through this exchange, so Edna started drumming her fingers on the Formica tabletop. Taking Edna's cue, the waitress slid her pencil back into her apron and said she'd be right back with their order.

Calvin was clearly infatuated, but Edna focused on her paper, pretending his stray glance didn't bother her. She knew it was harmless, and she herself had been known to be flirtatious from time to time, like with that new IT developer at school who happened to be an ex-jeans model. Not that he took her seriously when she complimented his new jacket while tucking her hair self-consciously behind her ear: not this forty-year-old mum with straggly hair and a wardrobe of shirt-dresses and comfortable shoes. Calvin coughed a little, adjusted his glasses, and reached for her hand. As she leaned across the table and kissed him lightly, she wondered once again how many times a day Calvin thought about her. It was a question that surfaced more and more frequently as the years passed. He had the nicest tasting lips of anyone she'd kissed, and each time she tasted that little hint of toothpaste and sweetness, it still took her by surprise. Even after fifteen years. Maybe how many times a day was not the right question, because the best answer would be one time: all the time.

The bagels turned out to be doughy in the centre even though they were toasted and crispy on the outside. Edna loved them. Her bagel was soft and seemed as if it could be chewed forever if you wanted, like a mouthful of cloud. This was no ordinary baked good. This was a kind of ecstasy. Calvin claimed he found them a heavy, unpleasant texture.

"So, okay, once we're done here we'll head to Central Park, then we need to have late afternoon drinks, and then we have to get gifts for the girls," she continued, pausing only when he reached over and wiped the corner of her cream-cheesy mouth with his thumb.

* * *

Edna has been keeping track of the little boy as he wanders back and forth across the departure lounge, trying to get a closer look at the bird. The sparrow's hops become increasingly frantic as it makes its way towards the corner of the room near the airline desk. Who could blame it? In the low-ceilinged room, it is well and truly trapped. Although each departure lounge is a separate glass box nestled beside other glass boxes on either side of a long open corridor, there are no windows to the outside to show the planes taking off or the light changing in the open sky. The most scenic view Edna has is of the Dunkin' Donuts on the other side of the secure area. The miracle of man-made flight was just beyond the exterior wall and her only view was of unreachable French crullers?

Alec approaches with his small, clumsy version of stealth, walking exaggeratedly on his tiptoes. As he gets closer, the bird hops farther away, and finally hides behind a metal garbage can. Now down on his belly, Alec crawls underneath the seats to spy on the bird, like a soldier infiltrating an enemy camp, and from where Edna sits she can see the bird twitch its head and look right at him for a second. As the boy crawls nearer, inching along the carpet towards her feet, Edna places her hand almost protectively on the small cardboard box sitting on the seat next to hers.

Cancelling the return leg of his journey was the most complicated thing she's had to do so far. The airline had refused to give her a refund because by the time she remembered to deal with his ticket there were less than 48 hours before the flight.

Most of the other paperwork could wait, they said, until she got back to Canada. She was surprised to find that cremated human remains were an allowable carry-on baggage item. The airline's policy made sense, she supposed. It could seem crass to relegate ashes to the hold. Still, what a relief to find them listed on the website as a permissible item, alongside strollers and small musical instruments. At least the cremation had been clear. Had been discussed. His wishes written down for the future. For a future more distant than now. When she read the guidelines on the airline's website, she felt as though they had been written just for her: anticipating her need for instructions and rules so that she didn't have to make any more phone inquiries. Sure, the real reason they listed it was probably to avoid having their employees deal with meltdowns. Not that she would have conducted herself that way. The airline staff were not to blame. She hadn't told the girls anything at all yet. How could she do that over the phone? And it wouldn't change anything, anyway. You can only do what you can do.

After their bagels, they went to Central Park to take a walk, and Edna felt the familiar disappointment of the week set in. It was a park, and parks were lovely, but it was really nothing remarkable as far as she could tell, unless what was notable about it was that the trees were able to survive in the smog of Manhattan. Like in any park, there were teenagers kissing in the bushes, and there were young mothers with running strollers jogging endless loops around the place. There were ice cream stands and little plaques explaining the flowers. She was sick of nature. They had the best of that at home: show-off sunsets and old-growth cedars. And those rowboats! How ridiculous.

"Maybe we should go and row one," he said.

Edna laughed. "What? Just so we can take pictures and the girls can make fun of us later? You're just trying to mess with the itinerary."

"Touché," said Calvin, pulling her in close and rubbing her shoulder.

All the activities she'd planned for them to do had taken on a kind of sarcastic edge, as though everything Tourist Edna had once earnestly wanted to do was suddenly a kind of parody. As they continued walking along the gravel path beside the lake, passing up the rowboats, Calvin nodded his head and rolled his eyes in the direction of a couple sitting under a tree with a picnic packed in mason jars. The twenty-something lovebirds were wearing almost identical clothes: skinny jeans, plaid shirts, and large black plastic glasses. There was a fedora on the grass beside the boy. When they were a safe distance away, Edna and Calvin started in on their saved-up observations for each other.

"Do you think we're hipsters? Or are we a little too old for that?"

"Definitely not." He stopped and kissed her on the cheek. "I don't get the whole hat thing."

She examined his faded slim jeans and his brown glasses and his hoodie. He really did dress like a hipster. Or they dressed like him. Edna ran her hands down her own belted sundress. She, on the other hand, would need some work, was not quite on the right side of cool. "I don't know. I think maybe we liked all the things that hipsters like before that kind of person really existed. They seem to be affecting what we felt for real. I do love how they're comfortable wearing animal tails under their jackets and disfiguringly large glasses. None of this worry about what's flattering."

"You'd look cute in a tail. I'll get you one." He tapped her cheekily on the bum and his hand lingered so that she could just barely feel it. What she wanted was for him to reach up her skirt. No level of planning could prepare her for this need. Forget rowboats; let's just do this thing. Go for a roll in the hay, maybe even get arrested.

But instead of grabbing him and pressing him up against a tree and showing him what she really wanted, she looked up at his big, green eyes and gave the string on his hoodie a mischievous tug. "Where would you find one?"

Alec's sister has opened up her carry-on, and neon bracelets and tank tops spill out onto the floor like an endless multicoloured scarf from a magician's sleeve. In this way she is like Edna's own girls, who seem to want to take up as much space as possible. She twirls her necklace around her fingers and stares up at the clock. "Seriously, what is going *on*?"

"It's just a delay," her mother replies. "I'm going to try to email Grandma and hopefully she'll get it on her phone. You know what she'll be like, out there at Arrivals with her cute little sign for us, like we wouldn't recognize her." The mother swipes her finger across the screen of her iPhone. "You bought too much stuff, Lily, " she chastises. "I don't even know how you did that in two hours at Filene's. Are you going to be able to close that suitcase again?"

"But we have receipts for everything so we're fine, right? We might just have to pay some taxes or something?"

"We should declare it all," her mother says, quieter this time, "and you can take Alec's share of the customs allocation. We'll just put the upper limit, I guess. Seems like you basically just bought the maximum. That's honest, in a way. The maximum."

Lily reaches down to untie her new Converse sneakers. "Hey, there's the bird again!" Lily follows the sparrow with her bright blue liquid-lined eyes. "I hope it doesn't shit on us." She pulls out her phone and holds it up, seeking a signal.

"Language, Lily. How many times?" The mother pauses. "Come to think of it, I've never considered robin poo before. Only pigeons. Or seagulls. Do you think it's smaller?"

"Probably." Lily inhales loudly and exhales through her teeth, making a whistling sound. The bird chirps back.

"Not a robin!" says Alec. "Robins are fatter and their tummies are red. Remember they had pictures in the bird book? Remember? Remember, Mum? Remember?"

"Okay, Birdface. Show off your expert knowledge," says Lily.

"Mum," says Alec, "why does she always have to be mean? Mum? Why?"

"She doesn't," says their mother, glaring at Lily.

There is a colossal snort, and everyone in the lounge turns to look at Lily's dad, who is sleeping with his mouth wide open. They've been waiting for nearly two hours now, and Edna's interest in the family has not abated. She has lost sight of the bird, but as she turns around to take the measure of the room she knows there's nowhere for the sparrow to go. How did it get in here in the first place? Edna traces the bird's journey through the airport as though it were just another passenger, and sees it coming in the front sliding doors. Through the check-in gates. Entering the secure area through the metal detector (not making it beep, of course). Riding down the escalator. Flying through the airless tunnels with their moving walkways. Past the domestic departures area and up three escalators, then in through the door to the lounge, where it must have landed, exhausted, on the carpet. Perhaps it got here by tucking itself away in a pocket or by perching on a rolling suitcase. Unless this is one clever bird, able to actually retrace its hops back through the lounge door, it's going to be stuck here with the rest of them.

"Excuse me." When she turns around again Alec is tapping her on the knee.

Before he can ask his question, his mum is up and apologizing to her and grabbing Alec by the wrist, dragging him back to their seats.

"Mum, I was just going to ask if we could borrow one of her puzzles so that you could do one to calm your nerves."

"People don't like to be bothered at times like these, Alec. Leave the nice lady alone." Alec's mum sits back down, still mouthing "I'm sorry" at Edna, and presses her index fingers to her temples. "Thanks for thinking of me, though, Al. That was a nice idea."

"It's fine," Edna starts to say, surprised at the hush of her own voice. She realizes she hasn't spoken out loud since she woke up this morning. Checked in online. Put her suitcases through the X-ray at security. Alec doesn't hear her. He sits and swings his legs beneath the chair since they don't reach the ground. Now both his sister and his dad are asleep.

"Mum, they're taking a napportunity," says Alec, and from the self-satisfied way he says it, Edna can tell that it's a family joke. *Dad takes any napportunity he can get.*

Alec's mother is now pulling an Edna and watching the security guards who are bickering by the airline desk. Edna hopes that's not how obvious she looks when she's living vicariously.

Alec is up and walking around again, searching for the bird. She considers getting up and helping him look, but she shouldn't leave her luggage, especially the box, unattended.

Alec suddenly stops and crosses his small legs theatrically. "I need to pee!"

"Congratulations, genius," Lily mumbles, her eyes still closed, "you're aware of your own human needs."

"Don't listen to her, Alec." The mum stands up and walks over to grab his hand. "It's good to think of it before we're in the air."

Alec sticks out his tongue at his sister and he and his mum follow the sign to the washroom.

Before Edna left on the trip, the boy from Brooklyn gave her tips for navigating the airport: "Just follow the signs. They have very good signage. The right kinds of signs are everywhere." He hadn't been able to explain to her what might happen if you were delayed like this. There was no sign to tell her how to spend these hours. Central Bus Station, yes. Baggage Claim, yes. Currency Exchange, yes. But why couldn't there be a sign for where she was now?

They carried on walking past the Diana Ross Playground where small children were learning to swing on the monkey bars, their patient teenaged babysitters holding tight to their chubby middles as their hands curled around the yellow metal bars.

"I miss the girls," said Calvin, watching the latest monkey bar student take her turn. "Now, but also when they were that age."

"Me too," said Edna. "Emma was so good at monkey bars. She'd have swung herself up and be walking on top of the bars by now."

"And Liz'd be worried about her, standing below like a spotter with her arms open wide."

"Too funny. They've always been sweet to each other." Edna watches as a small boy reaches his hands up to the sky, too little to quite grab onto the bars. "Okay, love, let's go. We don't want to miss our reservation!"

"Just give me a sec," he said, having moved on to reading a biography of Diana Ross etched in stone beside the entrance to the playground. "Just need a break here. You go on ahead. I'll catch up."

Edna glanced at her watch and realized that if they didn't hurry, all they would have done the whole day was stroll through Central Park and eat bagels, so she started to walk more briskly. She wanted to make sure that they'd be able to get to Tavern on the Green for a cocktail. She'd read in the guidebook that there were often celebrities there, so it was on her must-do list.

As she speed-walked along, pumping her arms, she looked up at the canopy of leaves above the path, at the branches grown into one another, their separate limbs blurring into a thick ceiling of foliage. She had read on centralparknyc.com that there were over 21,000 trees in the park, coniferous and deciduous species alike. She had even browsed the Tree Database in preparation for their day and there were sample photographs in a folder in her purse. Above her the bark was gruff and black and the leaves a pure spring green.

"American Elm," she said aloud, before turning back to see if Calvin had taken the hint and was catching up to her.

No, he had fallen back. Fallen.

She's disappointed when the family of four starts to pack up their things to catch their plane. The dad rouses from his snuffling slumber. He looks around for a moment, as if he's noticing the lounge for the first time, and then stands and hoists Alec, who lets out a squeak of surprise at being lifted, up over his shoulder. The mum and Lily gather their personal belongings. For some reason, Edna had assumed that they were waiting for the same flight she was. But of course there would be other delays and there would be gate changes. Why on earth should they have anything to do with her? She has been watching them without worrying about whether they'd notice. Because they won't. She knows this. They won't look at her. Maybe if she was wearing a tail . . . No. They still wouldn't look. They seem sweet in their impatience with each other. The way the wife nudged her husband to wake him without taking her eyes off the kids.

She tells herself to stop. This is not the place. Not the place to be thinking about his snoring, how quiet the hotel room had been without it. You can only do what you can do. The little boy seems worried about the bird with the kind of intensity that only children or activists worry about animals. But she has been eavesdropping, and she has a terrible habit of not only listening in but staring as well. It had embarrassed Calvin, her lack of subtlety.

"One of these days," he'd say, "someone is going to notice you." Used to say.

But how could she not pay attention to everyone else when she was on her own? She isn't ready for it all to be real yet. Isn't, in fact, prepared to even get on the plane. More to the point, to descend, to land. To walk down the gangplank to the Arrivals terminal, to see the girls waiting amidst all the drivers and anxious lovers at the gate. To say . . . what? They would have spent these last few days picturing her and Calvin in New York as she herself had once done: Just imagine! Mom and Dad in front of the Empire State Building, or rowing in Central Park. She should have bought the Yankees jersey for Emma. But there hadn't been enough time. If only she could just stay inside this other family's life for a little while longer. Or take herself back further, to the two of them standing in the park by the rowboats. But she isn't in either of those situations. Staring up at the fluorescent airport lighting, she feels as if she has fallen out of time altogether. Isn't it funny, she thinks, that this suspended animation is as much a part of life as every other day. Somehow, waiting here feels like it shouldn't count towards her time in the world, like it should come for free. Edna is a thoughtful purchaser. A keeper of receipts. She should be able to return these minutes and get her time back. Their time.

She closes her eyes for a moment too long and feels her seat begin to wobble. She might lean to the side and not be able to right herself.

She should do something, maybe get back to the puzzle, but sudoku is strange. Why a numbers game with no arithmetic? She counts instead, first in integers, then through the primes, then the squares and square roots, cubes and cube roots. What is the cube root of nine? Too easy. "Comprehensive" had been the doctor's word for the stroke. Like a study guide. An exam. Like the lessons Edna gives on trigonometric functions. In the corner of the room, the bird takes off: a shock of wings. It balks and flutters at the glass divider between one departure gate and another. Like that. Just like that.

ACKNOWLEDGEMENTS

To everyone at McClelland & Stewart and Random House of Canada, especially my editor, Anita Chong, for giving so much time, energy, and enthusiasm to the book. To the CBC Literary Prizes and the Canada Council for the Arts, to everyone at PEN International and PEN Canada, and to the Canadian Authors Association. To Nelson Adams for hosting the Random House team at the Massey College Press, and to Andrew Roberts, who came up with the inspired letterpress-style book design.

To the wonderful colleagues and students with whom I've had the pleasure of working over the past few years at the University of Toronto, the University of Reading, the Ontario College of Art and Design University, and the Modernist Archives Publishing Project. To Massey College, where much of this book was written. To John Fraser and Elizabeth MacCallum, for their unending generosity.

To my dear friends, especially those who cheered my writing on in various ways: Adele Allen, Tony Antoniades, Richard Bedell, Charlie Boss, Peter Buchanan, the Cherries, Alex Chester, Laura Christensen, Jimmy Clowes, Fiona Coll, Sarah Copland, Amy Cullen, Kellie Davis, Michael Dewar, James Dufton, Lindsey Eckert, Sarah Fornace, Ingrid Frater, Paul Furgale, Jeremy Hanson-Finger and everyone at Dragnet and the EW Reading Series, Letitia Henville, Eneli Holmes, Heather Jackson, Heather Jessup, Katy Knight, Thea Loberg, George Logan, Susan MacDonald, Jennifer McDermott, Nick Mount and the Lit for Our Time 2012–13 crew, Dan Newman, Shona Patterson, Rebecca Payne, Alex Peat, Harriet Phillips, Chelsea Phipps, Erin Piotrowski, Laura Potter, Zani Showler, Anne Simpson, Sean Starke, Robyn Uhl, Tom Wells, Michael Winter and the chip butty crowd, and Terence Young and the Writing 12 class at SMUS. To Aidan, Marjorie, and Gráinne O'Hogan for welcoming me into their family. To Jim Battershill and Dennis Barnard, who live on in these stories.

To Andrew Battershill, for being my first reader and my brilliant lil' bro. To Kelly Barnard and Peter Battershill, the best mum and dad in the whole wide world. To Cillian O'Hogan, *sine quo non.*

Thank you.

The epigraph is quoted from the e. e. cummings play *Him* (New York: Boni and Liveright, 1927).

John Keats's "On Seeing the Elgin Marbles" is quoted from *Major Works*, ed. Elizabeth Cook (Oxford: Oxford University Press, 2001).

The guide to the northern lights used by Edward in "The Collective Name for Ninjas" is Neil Davis's *The Aurora Watcher's Handbook* (Chicago: Chicago University Press, 1992). The article on the "Little Bang" parenting theory to which Jess refers is "Little Bang Parenting Theory: It All Begins with a Toy Gun" by Monica Hesse in the *Washington Post* (Saturday, November 11, 2007).

"Circus" first appeared in a slightly different form in *enRoute Magazine* in 2008.

The Latin in "Brothers" is quoted from Horace, *Ode* 1.9.5–8. *Q. Horati Flacci Opera*, ed. F. Klingner (Leipzig: Teubner, 1959).

I have taken some liberties with the particulars of luge life and have added a fictional Canadian team to the Vancouver 2010 Olympics in "Two-Man Luge: A Love Story." Aerodynamic booties really exist, though.

The phrase "quite everydaylooking" appears in James Joyce's *Finnegan's Wake*, ed. Jeri Johnson (Oxford: Oxford University Press, 1993).

A NOTE ABOUT THE TYPE

Circus has been set in Albertina MT, a digitized typeface created by Frank E. Blokland at the Dutch Type Library and based on original matrices drawn by Dutch typographer and calligrapher Chris Brand. Originally issued for photocomposition by Monotype in 1965, the typeface failed to catch on in its own time. A collaboration between Brand and Blokland in the mid-1990s saw the revival of an expanded and refined Albertina.